Me Jane

Larry was late. Everything was ready, and I'd got enough mascara on to keep a locomotive running smoothly – that's what Mum said, anyway. My heart was thundering away as if it would split my ribs. What if he didn't come? What would Mum think? How could I ever look my friends in the face?

The front doorbell rang. I kind of lurched out to answer it and banged my head on the doorpost. Then I had to pretend I wasn't on tenterhooks as I opened the door. I madly tried to pull on an expression of casual, carefree oh-hello-it's-you, like a sort of invisible pullover. But it got stuck over my ears.

"Lerro Harry!" I gasped. It wasn't a good start.

Sue Limb

Me Jane

Lions Tracks

An Imprint of HarperCollins*Publishers*

First published in Great Britain by Orchard Books 1989
First published in Lions Tracks
in association with Orchard Books 1991

Lions Tracks is an imprint of
the Children's Division, part of
HarperCollins Publishers Ltd,
77 Fulham Palace Road,
London W6 8FB

Set in Linotron Garamond

Phototypeset by Input Typesetting Ltd, London
Printed and bound in Great Britain by
William Collins Sons & Co. Ltd, Glasgow

Any good bits in this book were provided
by the extremely brilliant pupils
of Sir William Romney's School,
Tetbury, Gloucestershire,
who worked the whole thing out
and to whom, with grateful thanks,
this book is dedicated.

1

Here it was. My birthday. Fifteen. My mum had promised that by the time I was fifteen, my hips would've slimmed right down. But they hadn't. I bumped the right one on the bathroom doorpost as usual. It's black and blue. The hip, not the doorpost. I think one day I won't be able to get through the door at all. My mum says don't be daft, it'll all melt away. But nothing melts away from me. Except Larry Payne.

Larry Payne's really — but I mustn't start drooling about him. He's two classes above me at school, and I'm — but I mustn't. Anyway now I'm fifteen I'm going to ignore him. I've had enough pain and anguish. The thing is, he doesn't even know I exist. Just as well, says Ginger Mike, or it'd give him nightmares.

Ginger Mike is one of my mates. He's a tall guy with glasses, I've got a photo of us all by my bed, and Ginger Mike is standing at the back. The top of his head's missing, because Wayne's dad took the photo and he's not very good with cameras. Actually I think Ginger Mike looks better without the top of his head. I must remember to say so next time he needs a telling-off.

Wayne and Lorette are in the photo too, wearing Greenpeace T-shirts. Lorette is my best friend and Wayne is her brother. He's in the same class as

Larry Payne and he's always teasing me, threatening to tell Larry Payne that I'm crazy about him, that kind of thing. Some people think Wayne looks a bit like Michael Jackson but I don't think so. Wayne's no use at being bad, either. He can't stop being nice however hard he tries. He's stuck with it.

I got birthday cards from Ginger Mike, Wayne and Sudeshna. Sudeshna is really beautiful. She looks like some kind of Indian princess. Her dad keeps a corner grocery store, lucky thing! It must be great having a whole shop of your own. My mum's always running out of things. Really basic things like bread and tea. When I complain she says, "You ought to try being a single working mum!" Then I feel guilty. She's great, really, my mum.

I didn't have much of a birthday breakfast, though, because we'd run out of cereal and milk and eggs. Anyway I was late for school. Mum was still in the bathroom so I screamed, " 'BYE!" up the stairs. It made the doorbell tubes sort of vibrate. My voice is really much too loud. Maybe if I had a husky kind of whisper, Larry Payne would notice me. I practised whispering huskily all the way down the road.

Lorette was waiting at the bus stop. She looked angry and somehow magnificent with it. When I'm angry I just look angry.

"Where've you been?" she demanded. "I had to let two buses go by. We're gonna be really late, Jane."

"Sorry, sorry, sorry!" I murmured, hiding under

my English file. "Don't yell at me, Lorette. It's my birthday."

"Good job and all. Otherwise I'd brain you. Happy Birthday. At least it's not raining."

"Yeah. I'm going to sunbathe at lunchtime. Get a tan."

"Sunbathe? Cloudbathe, you mean."

Lorette looked up and the grey sky flashed in her brown eyes. It was all right for her. She was brown and beautiful all the year round. And had a fantastic figure. And could run faster than any other girl in school. Whereas me — well, I'm fat, slow, and my skin's the colour of porridge. In fact, if Lorette wasn't my best mate, I'd hate her guts.

"Here comes the bus. We're still gonna be late. You do the explainin' to old Fishface."

Not one bus but three came storming down the road. They always travel in threes, the number 73s. We reckon it's so they won't get scared. Safety in numbers. After all, the things that go on round our way, even a London bus would turn pale.

On the bus, Lorette gave me my present. It was a kohl eye pencil in a new colour — a dark sparkly green.

"Hey, it's terrific." I drew a heart on my hand. "I really like this green. It's sort of evil. Do you think it'll make me look like Emerald Storm?"

Emerald Storm is this fantastic lead singer in a group called *Hysteria*. Her eyes are all outlined in black like an Egyptian queen.

"You look more like the keyboard player."

Lorette is very quick with her put-downs. And man, when she puts you down, she puts you right

9

down, so your nose is practically on the pavement.
She's incredibly strong, too. She does a lot of training for her running and she really tries to live a pure
life, if you know what I mean. Even her mind's not
all that dirty. Not compared to me, anyway. My
mind's like the corporation dump.

I drew a green arrow through the heart on my
hand. Then I put a pair of initials on one side of
the arrow: J.W. Mine. Jane Watts. On the other
side I wrote L.P. For Larry Payne. Lorette looked
down at my hand and gave a sort of weary sigh.

"Do you think I should have a tattoo, Lorette?"

"I think you should have your head examined."

We were late, of course. Mrs Fisher gave us one of
her very best sulphuric acid smiles. Actually I like
her in a way — for a teacher — but she's really
sarky. "Her sarcasm," Ginger Mike says, "could
strip the varnish off a cupboard door at fifty
yards." He talks a lot like that. We don't mind.
We're used to it.

"Lorette and Jane. Late again." It sounded like
a poem.

"Sorry, Mrs Fisher, but it's my birthday."

"I see, Jane. Emotional blackmail, eh? All right.
I surrender. But if you're late again tomorrow . . . "

Her eyes went narrow like slits. She was very
good at menace. I think she used to be an SS guard
in a previous life. Obergruppenführer Fischer. It
even sounds right. Impressed? I'm taking German,
see. I failed my school exams last time, but that
was because my ears had gone septic.

We sat down. Most of the gang were lounging

around in their chairs, picking at their desks or doodling on the covers of books. Sudeshna gave me one of her most beautiful smiles.

"Happy Birthday, Jane!" she whispered. Honestly, she's so beautiful, it hurts. "I'll give you your present at break."

Ginger Mike was reading a science fiction book. He didn't even look up. Mark Stitchfield and Tony Williams started thumping each other. They're so immature. I suppose when they learn to talk they won't need to thump each other so much but Lorette says that right now it's the only way they have of communicating.

Twenty minutes this "class counselling period" lasts. Mrs Fisher takes the register. At first she used to try and counsel us, but she soon gave up because the boys kept laughing. Now she takes aspirins and does bits of her Physics marking. She doesn't mind us talking as long as we keep it quiet. Most of us do our last night's homework, but on this particular day I'd left my books at home, what with the excitement of my birthday.

"What did your mum give you?" whispered Sudeshna.

"A record token."

"Oh, great! What are you going to get with it?"

The bell rang, and my heart gave a little skip. It was Biology first lesson, and we had to walk past the sixth-form block. That was Larry Payne territory. I might see him. I wiped the heart off my hand with a bit of tissue. I'd heard of wearing your heart on your sleeve but this was ridiculous.

"I've worked out that Fishface is an intergalactic

11

secret agent," said Ginger Mike in my ear. "It's the way she crosses her legs. And she teaches Physics, so she's obviously spying on our earth technology. We'll have to watch her carefully in future and keep Washington informed of her movements."

I wasn't listening. We were nearly at the sixth-form block, and my heart was hammering away so hard I could feel it in my armpits. Would Larry Payne appear? I looked everywhere for his tall figure, his wavy black hair, his glinting blue eyes. Instead Lorette's brother Wayne sidled up. He's in the sixth form, too — going to be an engineer, he reckons.

"Hi, Jane! Happy Birthday! How about a kiss? Just to celebrate, you know."

"Gerroff, you sex maniac! And listen . . . is Larry Payne here today?"

"Sure, he's here. Somewhere. Shall I ask him if he wants to come an' give you a birthday kiss, too?"

"No, no! Don't be daft! Shut up, Wayne! Don't you dare say anything to him or I'll never speak to you again!"

I was blushing so hard, the whole school looked red. Wayne just laughed, ruffled my hair and sailed away.

I wish he wouldn't do that — ruffle my hair. It plays havoc with my spikes. It takes me ages with the setting gel to get them right and then Wayne comes along and messes them up. "Hey, little hedgehog!" he calls me sometimes. I wouldn't mind if Larry Payne mussed my hair or called me little hedgehog. But he looks straight through me, and his eyes are cold as lasers.

Biology was a riot, as usual. I mean literally. Mr Spicer's such a weed, I don't think he could control a couple of nuns saying their prayers. Five minutes of Spicer and they'd be throwing their rosaries about and bashing each other over the head with their Bibles. And as for us, the dreaded 4R — well, Ginger Mike says the Ministry of Defence has named a secret weapon after us. It's a nerve gas called 4R. It destoys all human life within a radius of five hundred miles. Just like we do. You ask the teachers. Well, ask Spicer anyway.

"Today we're going to study the human respiratory system."

"Is it dirty, sir?"

"Please sir, what's that in the bottle on your bench?"

"Did you sick it up in the night, sir?"

"WILL YOU BE QUIET! As I said, the human — er — STOP THAT, WILLIAMS! Er . . . Here we have a life-size model of a pair of human lungs."

"We done lungs last week, sir. You said this week we was going to do knockers."

"WILLIAMS, I WON'T TELL YOU AGAIN! Now the rest of you just PAY ATTENTION! And open your books at page 105."

"Please, sir, my book stops at page 104."

"Please sir I ent got a book no more. A zebra ate it on the way to school."

"I shall ignore these infantile remarks. On page 105 you will find a diagram of the human respiratory system. WILLIAMS, GET OUT! I'VE HAD ENOUGH!"

"Have you really, sir? I can't get enough, myself. 'Ow do you manage it?"

I'll draw a veil over the rest of the lesson. It would be the kindest thing to do. Short of offering Mr Spicer compulsory retirement and a villa in Majorca. What I can't understand is, why don't blokes like him get a nice quiet job going round reading people's meters or something? Instead of locking themselves away all day with a gang of hooligans and nutters like us? Or at least, that's what we turn into when Spicer's around.

"Spicer," murmured Ginger Mike in my ear as we crossed the yard forty minutes later, "turns into a werewolf at night and goes round the streets of Islington eating the hearts of virgins. We are his punishment. By day he must pay the price."

I didn't listen. I was looking for Larry Payne. I didn't see him at lunchtime, either. And it was too cold to sunbathe. Instead, Lorette, Sudeshna and me found a cosy little corner in the cloakrooms and Sudeshna brought out a great pile of chocolate bars from her dad's shop.

"Here, Jane — Happy Birthday."

She gave me a box all wrapped up in paper with roses on it. Inside was a bottle of Mystery Lagoon toilet water. We all put a bit behind our ears.

"You're supposed to put it on your pulse points, right?"

"Where's your pulse points, then, Lorette?"

"On your wrists and stuff. And behind your knees. And in your groins."

"I'm not putting any on my groins! Don't be daft!"

We all ate Sudeshna's chocolate bars. Lorette didn't really want to because of her training, and I didn't really want to because of my hips, but Sudeshna's so quiet and gentle we don't really like to offend her.

"Delicious!" said Lorette, wincing because the chocolate had hit her bad tooth.

"Yummy!" I added, feeling my hips quietly expanding. It's really fast-acting stuff, that chocolate.

"Thanks, Su. Only don't keep bringing it every day, really. You'll spoil us. We'll get addicted."

"Oh, no," Su smiled. "It's all right. My dad says so."

On the bus on the way home the sun came out for about five minutes. Lorette had stayed behind after school to do training, and Sudeshna had gone to the dentist, so I was on my own. The bus was warm and cosy and packed with people going home. It was such an ordinary day. And yet it was my birthday.

Then I had a sudden thought. Somewhere, among the mass of ordinary days — October the seventh, February the seventeenth, June the tenth — is a date on which, some day, you're going to die. And there it is, lurking among the other days, and you've got no idea, have you, that one day it's going to be your death-day? Weird.

You might have thought that would depress me, but it didn't. The thought of death doesn't terrify me. I think it's the beginning of the really *great* times. I'm looking forward to being able to fly around and disappear through walls and stuff like that. All the same, I don't want to die until I'm really old — thirty at least. I'm a bit worried about my hands. Sometimes they look a bit mottled and I'm afraid it might be the first symptom of a fatal disease.

I got off the bus outside the town hall and went into Fowl Fruit Shop. Actually it was originally called Fowler's but the e, r, and 's have dropped off the sign. Andy Fowler was in there, polishing away at his apples. But I had to go in.

"Hello," I said. "Who could be Fowler?" It was an old joke.

"Help, no, it's *her*. Look, would you mind going outside, love? One look from you and the fruit goes bad."

He was grinning at me all across his face. It's a strange bony kind of face, and he's got slanty green eyes and scrubby brown hair like a doormat.

"Give me a couple of oranges, please."

"Take them! Take whatever you want! Only get out! I can't bear it!" He pretended to hide behind a bag of potatoes.

I took two oranges, and held out thirty pence. He wouldn't take it, as usual. He'll never take my money. He just keeps mucking about and grinning all the time. It's really embarrassing when the shop's full of people. Luckily there was no one else around today.

"Come on, take it — or do I have to throw it at you?"

"Yeah, throw it at me! If you can hit me on the nose I'll give you a pineapple."

I threw both coins at him. One hit him on the shoulder, the other on the knee.

"Have a pineapple anyway. This one. I was keeping it specially for you, 'cos it's gone off."

He shoved a pineapple into my bag.

"What's up with you today, anyway?" he went on. "You've got a face like a wet weekend. I mean even more than usual."

"Oh, nothing. It's just my birthday, that's all. And it's just great being told you look like a wet weekend on your birthday."

"Your birthday, is it? What presents did you get?"

"A record token. And some eyeliner. And some toilet water."

"Blimey. If I'd known, you could have had some of my toilet water too. Only the flush won't work properly."

"Ho ho. Very witty. Well, I must be going. I don't want to hang about here — I might catch something."

"Ah well. I hope you choke on the pineapple! And cheer up! Tell you what — I'll give you a bag. You could put it over your head. That'd improve the view for all of us."

I picked up a Granny Smith apple and shoved it into his mouth. He sank his teeth into it and growled like a dog. While he was struck dumb like that I made my escape.

Still, I felt he'd won that particular round. As I walked the last few yards to our flat, I felt a kind of sad, sinking feeling in the pit of my stomach. It was something to do with Fowler's Fruit Shop. I always felt like that after I'd been there. It was a bit like the first stages of food poisoning.

As soon as I got in, the phone rang. It was Ginger Mike. You can always tell it's Ginger Mike because he never says who he is.

"See you in the cemetery in an hour," he hissed. "The usual place."

2

Mum hadn't got home from work yet, so I quickly made myself some sardines on toast and a banana. I didn't actually *make* the banana, of course, but you know what I mean. I hate sardines, but Lorette says you have to eat lots of fish because it's good for your bones. I like bananas, though. They take away the taste of the fish.

I put an orange in my pocket to take to the cemetery. I thought I might get Ginger Mike to have half of it. Lorette says he looks as if he's seriously short of Vitamin C, but I think he looks as if he's packed with it. For a start, he's got bright red hair. Just the colour of carrots and oranges and all that Vitamin C type food. But I know Lorette must be right, because she's gone into Nutrition in a big way. In fact, sometimes I think she's never managed to come out properly the other side.

I got into the cemetery the usual way — down Summertown Road and over the wall. They lock the cemetery at five, which is great, because it means we get it all to ourselves. It's a huge, rambling, overgrown place. The trees tower over you so that in places it's just like a forest. There's old tombs everywhere, going right back for hundreds of years — and most of them are choked with weeds and nettles and shrubs. You can see squirrels running about up in the branches, and all sorts of birds. We saw a woodpecker once, and a big white owl blinking at us. He looked just like a cat. It's great, the cemetery. It's the best place there is. It's better than the park, because there are no adults to bother you.

Ginger Mike was in the usual place. We've got this little kind of den behind a really big tomb. It's got a shocking great marble angel on it, pointing up to heaven, with her long hair streaming in the wind. She's got a piece of her wing missing. I expect she had a bit of a close shave with a Boeing 737.

"Hey, Mike, are angels blokes or girls?"

"They're hermaphrodites. A bit of both."

"Or a touch of the other," I giggled. Ginger Mike didn't. His giggle-threshold is quite high. He reached inside his pocket.

"I've got a little something for you, Jane. For your birthday." He held a little white pill in the palm of his hand.

"What is it?"

"The very best."

"Yes, but the very best *what*? Where did you get it?"

"I don't reveal my contacts. I am a man of discretion. Take it or leave it."

I took it. I knew it was only something like aspirin. It always is. Ginger Mike likes to set himself up as this ace dope dealer but all he ever really does is raid his mum's bathroom cabinet. He listens to a lot of Beatles records and early Dylan. He's a very old-fashioned guy, really.

I remember the only time he ever actually took anything real. It was during the glue-sniffing craze.

He brought some glue and a bag. Lorette wouldn't do it because she disapproved; Sudeshna was too scared, and wild horses couldn't drag me into that sort of thing. So in the end Ginger Mike was the only one to sniff it. Then he went behind a tree and was sick. Lorette said it served him right. She can be a little hard sometimes.

Anyway, I took the pill. I could tell right away, as soon as it hit my tongue, that it was an indigestion tablet. It had that peppermint-and-chalky taste.

"What will this do for me, then, Mike?"

"Listen, Jane Watts, this will just *do for you*. OK? Enough said?"

He lay back and looked up at the sky.

"The light evenings are coming, Mike."

"Yeah. Why don't we stay out all night on Midsummer Night?"

"I tell you why not. Because our Biology exam is the very next day."

"Ah, what the hell. We're all going to fail it anyway. Spicer's classes always fail."

"Why don't they give him the sack?"

"You can't sack teachers. Not unless they've got their hands in the till — or up some old girl's skirt."

I tried to imagine Spicer doing either of these, but he didn't seem human enough, somehow.

Above our heads, clouds drifted past, tinged faintly with gold. It was a nice evening, after all. Our angel was catching the sun, and it made her nose shine. We liked our tomb. It was some old Italian woman's: her name was on it. CARA GIOVA-

NEZZA. She died in 1913. Cara Giovanezza. Italian's a really nice language. Not like German. In German you practically have to rupture your tonsils just to say Good Morning.

Cara Giovanezza . . . she'd have been young in, say, the 1870s. Had she ever lain on her back and looked up through trees at the sun? Had she had big hips? Had she longed for some Larry Payne look-alike to give her the nod? Had she been in love? You couldn't tell, from her tombstone. After her name it was all blurred.

There was a sudden crash and a thump, and Lorette and Wayne landed with us — or practically on us.

"Hey, man, there's goin' to be a big party down the park next month. *Youth Joy* is going to play — and *Hysteria*."

"I bet it'll rain."

"They'll play anway. They can play on the bandstand. It's covered."

"What's it all in aid of?"

"It's a Greenpeace rally. Anti-nuclear. There's going to be stalls and stuff and speeches an' that, right? And we're all goin' to go and join so we can demonstrate."

Lorette really likes organising. I gave a groan.

"It's all a waste of time, this Greenpeace stuff. They'll never take any notice of us. And there's not going to be a nuclear war anyway."

"Doesn't have to be a war, Jane! Another Chernobyl could kill thousands of people. Trouble with you is, you got no social conscience."

"Little hedgehog!" grinned Wayne. "I know

what you'll do if the bomb drops. Roll yourself into a ball."

"Do you think there'll be another Chernobyl, Mike? Or a nuclear war?"

"If the Space Invaders don't get us first. ZAP! KERCHAW KERCHAW KERCHAW! Entire planet vapourised by Gamma X-lasers. Just like in *A Hitchhiker's Guide to the Galaxy*."

"You see, Jane, this is just the sort of male aggression that causes all the wars, right? Until the women have got control, nothin's ever goin' to improve."

"Women have got control — in this country anyway," grinned Wayne.

"She's not a real woman! She's just a man with tits. Everybody knows that. We gotta mobilise. We gotta get our act together. We've gotta change the world while we've still got one to change."

I began to wonder if Lorette had trained quite hard enough after school. She seemed to have much too much spare energy. Wayne yawned and gave me a gleaming smile. His brown eyes were restful, really nice. Not like his sister. Lorette's always on the buzz. Wayne is sort of cool and loose.

"The band's gonna be really good, anyway. You comin', Jane?"

"I dunno."

I felt restless. I did want to do something, but not all this marching and protesting and listening to boring old speeches. It all made me want to go to sleep. I agreed with it all, of course, but I just wished they'd get on with it without me.

A quiet stealthy step on the other side of the

tomb, and Sudeshna arrived. We were surprised. She doesn't often manage to get away in the evenings. Her parents are really strict, especially now the exams are coming up. She spread a plastic mac carefully on the ground and then sat on it; then she got out the chocolate. Luckily, Wayne and Mike ate two bars each, so Lorette and I escaped with just the odd bite.

"Hey, you guys," I began at last, thinking, what the hell, I really have to sort this out in my mind, "what do you reckon happens after you die?"

"Not a lot!" grinned Wayne. "It's curtains. That's it. That's your lot. Down among the dead men. You join the carbon cycle."

"What's that?"

"It's like when animals eat other dead animals, or plants grow out of dead bodies. I mean, see this tree? Its roots go right down into what'shername's coffin, I bet."

"Cara Giovanezza?"

"Yeah. Well, this old tree's roots sure as anything must've, like, fed off her in some way."

"You're disgusting, Wayne!"

"It's not disgusting," I said. I rather liked the idea of turning into a tree. But I had to know about the Afterlife.

"Don't you believe in spirits and souls and things, then, Wayne?"

"No, he don't!" snapped his sister. "He's simple minded. Scientists are so stupid. They only believe what they can see!"

"What do you believe, then, if you're so sophisticated?" retorted Wayne. "I notice you don't go to church any more with Mum and Dad."

"Yes, I do sometimes, so! I know I've got a soul. I feel it all the time. And when I die it's going to live on, somewhere. Somehow."

"We believe —" Sudeshna began quietly, and we all immediately stopped shouting at each other and listened. It was quite an event when Su said anything. " — We believe that you get born again in a different body." I liked the sound of that. I hoped my next body would have slim hips. "If you've been good you can come back again as a superior type of person," Sudeshna went on. "And if you've been bad you might come back as an animal."

"How long does it take?" asked Wayne. "I mean, are you born again right away, the very next minute after you die? Or do you get a bit of a rest and a cup of tea first?"

"No, I don't believe in all that Reincarnation," said Lorette. "It's not Christian, right?"

"Well, of course not," smiled Sudeshna, blushing.

"I like the idea," I said. "I want to come back as a bird. A big bird. Like an owl."

"BAM!" Mike took aim and shot me off my perch.

"Shut up, for God's sake, Mike," said Lorette, "or somebody'll hear us in here and ring the police."

"Police?" sneered Ginger Mike. "Let 'em come. OK Old Bill, say your prayers! BAM PARA-PARA-PARA-PARA-WHA — BAM!!!"

"Hey man, Lorette's right," said Wayne softly.

25

"You goin' to bring the law in on us and ruin everything."

Mike was quiet. He listens to Wayne.

"Death?" Mike said quietly to himself. "Not tonight, dear, I've got a headache."

Conversation drained away, and we became more aware of the birdsong around our heads. Sudeshna polished her bracelets and smiled shyly to each of us in turn. Mike was whistling to himself in a very soft, out-in-orbit sort of way. Lorette's brow was all screwed up and I could see she was still trying to solve the world's problems.

Suddenly I became aware that Wayne was looking at me. I looked back. But there was something new in his eyes. I caught on them like barbed wire, then managed to look away again, and felt strange. *Wayne*? Surely not. I was his little hedgehog. He didn't feel, well, like *that* about me, did he? I didn't dare to look again. A raindrop hit my head.

"Hey! It's raining!" I scrambled up, and the others slowly stirred.

"I got to go too," Sudeshna picked up her mac and put it on. "My dad's going to kill me as it is."

I sneaked a look at Wayne. He seemed ordinary again, thank goodness. He was just my mate, like Ginger Mike. It would spoil it all if any of that sort of thing started creeping in.

We jumped over the wall and parted, and I walked home and looked at the wild sunset colours of the sky. It hadn't rained, after all. There had been just that one drop, smack on my brow. The weather didn't seem to know what it was doing.

Up ahead outside the pub, a figure loomed in

the dusk. He had a dog on a lead. It was Andy Fowler. Oh no!

"When's your birthday party, then?"

"I'm not having one. And even if I was, you wouldn't be invited."

"Well, that's a relief." His grin flashed. The dog started to snuffle at me.

"Get your horrible dog to leave me alone. I hate dogs. Especially yours."

"He can't help himself. It's that toilet water of yours. It makes you irresistible — to dogs."

We both stood silent and awkward for a moment. I wanted to thank him for the pineapple, but somehow I couldn't.

"We've just been in the cemetery — talking about death."

"Who's we?"

"Me and my mates."

"Who's your mates?"

"Wouldn't you like to know?"

"Couldn't care less."

Another silence. I was beginning to feel slightly queasy.

"I'm going," I blurted suddenly. "I'm late already."

And I ran off.

It's funny, but as I was running home, two tears sprang from my eyes and the whole street went blurred. As I got in, Mum looked up from the telly. Her face was really pale.

"Jane! Where have you been? Are you all right? What's the matter?"

"Nothing! I was just running and the wind made

my eyes water. What's up with you, though, Mum?
You look as though you'd seen a ghost."

"It's poor old Mrs Weldon next door. She was
attacked this evening. Poor thing. It was terrible.
I'm so glad you're home, love."

3

Have you ever seen an old lady with two black eyes? It's terrible. Poor old Mrs Weldon was pretty shaky on her pins even before the attack. Now she can hardly even walk round her flat without a stick. Mum goes round every day after work to see how she is, and she gets Meals on Wheels for lunch. But sometime in the afternoon there'd been a knock on her door, and these two blokes wearing balaclavas had pushed their way in and said, "All right, Grandma, where's the money?" And when she refused to tell them, they'd punched her. Punched an old lady who can hardly walk.

"I gave 'em a whack with me stick," she told me, as I made her her bedtime cocoa, "but I'm too old, Jane. I wish I'd been thirty years younger. Then I'd have given them a bleedin' good hiding. Pardon my French."

Mrs Weldon is a really colourful character. She used to work down the East End, in the markets. I gave her her cocoa and made her a hot water bottle and told her if there was anything more we could do, to ring. Then I went back home. I heard her locking and bolting the door behind me.

"How could they do it?" I burst out at Mum, who was watching TV and sewing buttons back on to my school shirt. "I mean, she's a helpless old lady. Mum! How could they?"

"Some people are just like that," said Mum, biting off a thread. "It takes all sorts."

On the TV, there was a car chase through some American streets. Then the cars crashed, and the blokes jumped out and started a fist fight. BAM! THUMP! POW! KICK! It was as bad as one of Ginger Mike's fantasies.

"Turn it off, Jane," said Mum, searching for another button. "I hate all this violence."

I did. The room was suddenly so quiet, you could hear the carpet breathing. I sighed.

"But — but what can we do about it?" I asked. Mum shrugged. She wasn't being very helpful. She was tired, you could tell by the way the corners of her mouth turned down.

"The best thing you can do is keep right out of it," she warned. "I don't want you being all heroic and getting into trouble. Men are stronger than us. You must be careful, Jane."

"Are you saying we should just stand by and let them get away with things like this?" I shouted. Mum winced, sighed and put her sewing down for a minute.

"It's not that, love. I mean, it's just the way things are, nowadays. We live in a violent world. I hate the thought of you getting hurt, Jane."

She reached out for my hand and I knelt down by her chair and gave her a big hug.

"Don't be frightened, little Mum," I whispered into her shoulder. She always smells nice. It's not scent or moisturiser or anything, it's just Mum's skin. I remember it from when I was ever so little and I used to sit on her knee. We have this joke, now that I'm bigger than her, that I've got to look after her. She worries too much. "Don't worry. I'll take care of you. Your great big daughter is here."

"Girls are vulnerable, though, Jane," she said. "Really, sometimes when you're late home I — " She didn't finish the sentence. But I knew what she was thinking. "I know I shouldn't, but I really worry about you staying out late."

I didn't like the sound of that. Time to change the subject — and fast.

"Come on, Mum!" I got up and smiled coaxingly. "How about a nice hot cup of tea with some of those salty biscuits? You stay here and put your feet up — I'll get it ready."

Mum smiled, and picked up my school shirt again. It's dreadful, the way those buttons keep bursting off. I must go on a diet.

As I made the tea, I thought about Mum and all her fears. She's scared of everything. She won't go out at night unless she can afford a taxi, and she hardly has any fun. It's six years since my dad cleared off so her life must be incredibly boring. And she's terrified of every little thing. At the moment it's food poisoning. First she wouldn't buy eggs, then cheese, then those yummy samosas from Sudeshna's dad's shop. Now she's bought us a water filter.

"Just think," Mum had said, staring at a glass of water one day, "it's been through eight pairs of kidneys before it even comes out of our tap."

That's exactly the sort of thing she thinks about all the time. Me, I prefer to wipe it out of my mind the minute I hear it — like a teacher wiping the blackboard.

Next time our gang was together, I told them about the attack on Mrs Weldon. Lorette's eyes got wider and wider and her lip trembled.

"We gotta do something about this, now!" she said. "That old lady was a victim of male violence!"

Ginger Mike seized a stick and pretended it was a Kalashnikov. He jumped to his feet and crouched, just like he'd seen in the movies, and sprayed an imaginary group of muggers with a hail of bullets.

"ZAKA ZAKA ZAKA ZAKA ZAK!"

"For God's sake, Mike, shut up!" yelled Lorette.

"Hey! I was wiping out the bad guys."

"But that's no good! You can't wipe people out. Even if they are bastards. You gotta change them."

Wayne laughed softly to himself and rolled over onto his back.

"You ain't never gonna change people, Lorette."

"Why not? People do change. If they realise the damage they've done. The trouble is, they never see it. If those guys who beat up Mrs Weldon had been taken back to see her, and talked to her and listened to her, they might've stopped feeling that what they did was so bloody clever."

"I know," said Ginger Mike. "Let's start a vigilante group. To protect people round here. Like those Guardian Angel people in the underground in New York. The subway, I mean. Then if anybody gets nasty — BAM!"

"What would you do if you were attacked, Lorette?" I asked.

"Run like hell," said Lorette with a grin.

Well, it was all right for her. She could run faster than anyone else in London, practically.

"What would you do, Sudeshna?"

Sudeshna smiled and shrugged.

"Pray."

The thought of Sudeshna being attacked was particularly horrible. If anyone ever did hurt her, I'd set Ginger Mike on them. Except we all knew that if it came to it, Ginger Mike would be useless in a fight. He was beaten up in the park about six months ago. These three big blokes stopped him, asked for his wallet, took his glasses off and stamped on them, and then punched him on the nose. We live just round the corner, so he came round to our place straightaway, with his nose bleeding all down his shirt, and trying not to cry.

"The trouble is, we're all so helpless!" I said, pulling up handfuls of grass and throwing them away in disgust. "My mum was saying how she gets worried whenever I'm out."

"So does mine," said Sudeshna.

"Right. In fact if there's any more attacks like this, I don't think she'll let me come out after tea, at all."

"Tell you what," said Wayne, sitting up and looking straight at me in a serious kind of way. "Why don't you do self-defence classes? My martial arts teacher does special sessions for girls. Down the community centre on Wednesday nights. Shall I find out about them for you?"

"Hey, that's a fantastic idea!" I was really grateful to Wayne. "Wayne, you're brilliant!"

"Not that you need self-defence, Jane," he grinned. "All you'd have to do is run at somebody with your head down. One glimpse of those spikes and he'd be off over the horizon!"

"Maybe I should do self-defence as well," pondered Ginger Mike. "But I don't think I'm the type. I think I'd better get really rich and hire a couple of bodyguards."

"How are you going to get really rich, Mike?" asked Sudeshna.

"Be a film director," said Mike, pretending to have a camera in his hand and filming us. "It's inevitable. A talent like mine cannot remain hidden for ever."

Then he put on a kind of horror film voice and stalked around us with the pretend camera focussed on us all the time. "*It was just an ordinary summer evening in the Bronx,*" he began. "*A group of kids were talking in the park. Little did they know the horror that lurked just around the corner. Hidden in the bushes, waiting for the night, was . . . THE THING!*"

And then he jumped on us with a bloodcurdling yell.

"It's a shame boys our age are so immature, isn't it, Jane?" asked Lorette pointedly. Wayne grabbed Mike, tied him up in a kind of knot, and sat on him. It was great, the way he did it.

"Hey! Wayne! Will I be able to do that to boys if I take this self-defence course?" I asked. He grinned at me for a moment, and his eyes started to dance in a funny kind of way.

"Sure," he said. "As long as you don't do it to me!"

I had to look away again, quick. I turned to Sudeshna.

"You must do this course, too, Su," I said. "We girls have got to learn how to defend ourselves!"

"I'm not sure if my dad will let me," sighed Sudeshna. She was right, as it turned out. He didn't.

Lorette came over to my place on Saturday, and we went to the chemist's. We were going to dye my hair Burgundy Glow. She was going to help.

"It'll be great!" I said, imagining myself with a Rich Shimmering and Glinting Burgundy Glow as promised on the packet. My normal hair colour's, well, mousy. In fact, it's more kind of gerbil-colour. It does look OK after I've washed it — for the first twenty minutes. But the thought of having hair that shimmered and glinted was very exciting. It might change my whole life. I read the instructions as we walked home.

"Wait!" said Lorette as we passed Fowler's Fruit Shop. "I gotta get some vitamins. Come on, Jane."

I whipped the Burgundy Glow hair stuff quickly into my bag. I didn't want Andy Fowler to tease me about that.

"So! What's new?" asked Andy, with a cheeky expression on his face. He nodded to Lorette. He knew her slightly, but he didn't take liberties with her like he did with me.

"I'm going on a self defence course," I said without thinking, and regretted it right away. Andy Fowler creased up.

"What, you? Self-defence? What for?"

"In case I'm attacked." It sounded a bit stupid, now.

"Blimey, I'm terrified! Will you be able to throw me over your shoulder or kick me on the eyebrows like in those martial arts movies?" Andy hid behind the till. Then his dad came out from the back of the shop.

"A pound of those black grapes, please," said Lorette.

"How's the running going?" asked Andy's dad. "You're that girl who won the area championships, aren't you?"

Lorette receives compliments gracefully. Whereas I — well, I never get any.

"There's a big meeting next month," said Lorette. "I'm training for that. Then they're going to pick the British Under 18 team to go to Rome."

Andy came out from behind the till and listened. Well, anybody would, wouldn't they? I felt proud of Lorette.

"You'd better try this then." He picked up a big orangey-pink fruit and slipped it into my bag. "Feed this to your sporty friend," he whispered to me. "It's a mango. Packed with vitamins. She needs feeding up. Muscle development. Remember! It's not for you. You don't need building up. You scare me stiff as it is."

I felt odd as we walked out.

"Lorette," I said as we crossed the road. "He said I was fat."

"What? You crazy or something, Jane? He never mentioned it."

36

"He did. Not in so many words. But that's what he meant."

As we walked up to the house, I realised how short and stumpy I looked, waddling along next to Lorette. She was so tall and graceful that beside her, I looked like one of the Seven Dwarfs. And Andy Fowler had noticed. If he thought I was too fat, what would Larry Payne think, if he ever noticed me? Not that he ever would, of course. Boys don't notice girls who waddle and have bums like bulldozers.

The funny thing was, I hadn't thought of Larry Payne for quite a while. And now he'd come back into my mind I'd started feeling miserable again. We got in, and I unpacked the Burgundy glow and the mango.

"Here's your mango," I said. "He meant it for you."

"Don't be daft, Jane! It was for you. I don't even know him."

I stared at the mango for a while, and then put it in the fruit bowl. There was a really deep sinking feeling in my stomach, like before an exam.

"Come on, Jane! Let's get this hair sorted out!" said Lorette.

Listlessly I picked up the packet of Burgundy Glow and opened it. The trouble was, whatever colour my hair was, I'd never be tall and slim and confident like Lorette. I didn't need a hair colorant. I needed a mind, body and soul transplant.

4

By the day of the Greenpeace fair, though, I felt
better. At lunchtime you could hear the throb of
music from the park. I was too excited to eat my
lunch.

"Don't worry, Mum!" I said, grabbing my
jacket. "I'll have something there."

"Oh dear — well, all right."

Mum didn't have a leg to stand on, really,
because we'd run out of bread again.

"Be careful, love!" she shouted, as I dashed out
and slammed the door. I'd tried to persuade her to
come as well, but she'd said she was too old for
that kind of thing. And she's not even thirty-eight
till October. Honestly!

I met the gang under the chestnut tree by the
loos. Ginger Mike was wearing a pair of luminous
pink rabbit's ears. They clashed horribly with his
red hair. Lorette was jiggling up and down in time
to the music. Wayne looked great in his white T-
shirt, old black leather jacket and faded jeans. Mind
you, he'd look good in a bin-liner. I wish he'd give
Ginger Mike some tips on how to dress. Sudeshna
had some new earrings, and they were tinkling
faintly in the breeze.

We walked round the park, looking at all the
stalls. The speeches were due to begin at half past
two, but there was lots going on already. There

were stalls selling jewellery, and badges, and antiques, and old clothes, and hamburgers. Gradually we broke up. Lorette went for a jog round the lake, Sudeshna got hooked on a jewellery stall, Ginger Mike found a stall selling old LPs and cassettes, and that left Wayne and me.

Wayne paused by a stall selling second-hand clothes. He went down the racks of old shirts, jackets and dresses. Then he pulled out an old dress made of sort of slithery blue material. He rubbed it between his fingers.

"Hey, Jane!" he said. "You should get this dress. It's really you."

I gawped. A dress like that, *me*? I hardly ever wore dresses at all. I tend to throw on a sweatshirt and jeans and that's it.

"God, no!" I shook my head and giggled. "I'm much too fat for that. I'd look terrible, Wayne."

Wayne held the dress up against me and looked me up and down.

"You're wrong there, sister," he said. "Fat? don't be stupid. You're just right. You should wear this sort of thing. Show off what you've got. You'd knock us all dead."

I stared into his brown eyes. He was laughing. Was he taking the piss? I felt the dress. It was silky against my fingers. I stroked it.

"Go on, try it on," he urged. "In the loos. You'd let her, wouldn't you?" he asked the owner.

"Sure," said the owner. "Go ahead."

"Oh, no, I can't!" I faltered. "I mean, I've got my trainers on and everything. It'd look all wrong. I'd have to have the proper shoes and things."

"Come on, Jane!" said Wayne, with his head on one side. He looks very appealing like that. He knows how to get round people. "I know you're shy. But just try it. You don't have to come out and show it to us. Just try it on in the loos, by yourself."

"But there aren't any mirrors in there," I said hastily.

"It's a great colour for you, too, that blue," Wayne went on, and the way he was looking at me made me feel hot all over. "Shows up your lovely white skin."

Lovely white skin? My skin had always been the bane of my life. I never go brown in the summer, only red and lumpy. And in the winter I'm so pale, people are always asking if I feel all right, and telling me I look ill. Nothing makes you feel ill quicker than someone telling you you look ill. And here was Wayne telling me my skin was lovely. He wasn't kidding either. I knew he meant every word of it. In a way it was terrific, it made me feel all excited inside. But I was scared too. I didn't feel safe with this new Wayne.

I hung the dress back on its rail, and shook my head. I wanted to start talking about something else.

"I'll think about it," I told the owner. "Thanks."

And I walked off. Wayne followed. He didn't say anything much for a while. In fact, we were both quiet, and awkward in a way. We were glad when Ginger Mike came up and showed us the cassette he'd bought.

"It's an old Bob Marley thing called 'Kaya'," he

said proudly. Then he plugged himself in to his Walkman and started dancing about. Ginger Mike dancing is quite a sight. Like a giraffe having a fit. And he sang along with Bob Marley at the same time.

Wayne and I sat down at the lake. In the middle of the lake is an island with trees on it.

"Look!" said Wayne suddenly, pointing. "A heron!" He put his other arm round my shoulders, to show me where to look. There, far away across the water, on the island, was a tall grey-blue bird with a long beak and stilt-like legs.

"Hey!" I breathed. "Brilliant!"

I love birds, and I'm glad Wayne's got such good eyesight. He was the one who saw the owl in the cemetery. He knows what all the species are, too. He's got books about them at home.

Mike was still prancing about listening to his Walkman. I wondered what to say next. I'd never been in this position before, wondering what to say to Wayne. But I was aware that he'd left his arm stretched along the back of the seat, sort of touching my shoulders — without actually being, well, draped round me. I wondered if he realised he'd left his arm there. I wished he'd take it away again, although my back seemed to like it. I'd have to give my back a good talking-to when I got home.

"Mike is an idiot, isn't he?" I said affectionately.

"He's a genius," said Wayne. "Hey, Mike!"

Mike stopped prancing and removed his head-phones.

"Yeah?"

"Why don't you go get us something to eat,

man? A couple of hot dogs or somethin'. I'm starving!"

He threw Mike a couple of pound coins and Mike ran off. He's totally obedient to Wayne. It's a good job Wayne's such a decent bloke, or Mike could go really off the rails. He's easily led.

Wayne's arm was still there, and my back was still enjoying it. A sort of glow spread along my shoulders. But I didn't go along with all this. I tried to tell my shoulders that Wayne was just a friend, one of my very best mates, and that was all. He wasn't my type, I knew he wasn't my type, and I mustn't give him the wrong impression because that could land us in a pretty awful mess and ruin our friendship for ever. But my shoulders just laughed. They were being very irresponsible.

Then, out of the blue, somebody big sat down next to me on the bench. BOOOOING! The bench kind of vibrated.

"Hi, guys!"

It was Larry Payne. LARRY PAYNE! I was so amazed, my head nearly fell off. Something deep inside me, a bit further down than my heart — sort of behind my tummy button — went up like a fireworks display. My knees trembled, my ears sang and sixteen different shades of red whizzed across my cheeks. Whilst I was trying to keep my body from falling apart, Wayne was introducing me to Larry Payne.

"You know Jane?" he said. Larry Payne grinned at me — AT ME! — and said, yeah, sure, he knew me by sight.

This was bad news, of course. I didn't like people

to know me by sight, because of the waddling and the big bum. But Larry Payne had grinned. Whilst I was trying to work out what sort of grin it was, he said,

"What are you two up to anyway?"

"Birdwatching," said Wayne quickly. Larry gave me a strange laugh.

"There was a heron on the island," I said. My voice sounded all odd and loud. Hell! I must remember to whisper huskily. We all looked at the island. The heron had gone. Wayne's arm had gone, too. Suddenly, in a few seconds, the whole world had changed. Here I was, talking to Larry Payne for the very first time.

"What do you think of it, then?" he asked, looking at me.

"What — this, like, fair thing?" I whispered huskily.

"What?" asked Larry Payne. I'd overdone the whispering.

"This — like, all the stalls and the bands and everything?"

"Yeah."

"It's great! We should have lots more things like this in the park. I mean, I've never seen so many people here. It's brilliant!"

"I don't think it's so great," said Larry Payne. "That band *Youth Joy* is a real no-no."

"What about Emerald Storm? Don't you go for her?" asked Wayne.

"Nah!" said Larry, staring at his trainers. They looked new. "Not my type. Too skinny."

43

"She's a great performer, though," I said, trying to hide my relief that he didn't like skinny girls.

"Hey!" said Wayne, looking over towards the bandstand. "I think it's time for the speeches, now."

He got up. Larry didn't move. He turned to me, looked at me for a brief moment, and then asked, "What sort of music do you like, then, Jane?"

Wayne hesitated.

"You comin'? To hear the speeches."

Time seemed to stand still for a minute: everything froze. Both guys were looking at me and it seemed suddenly unfair, as if I was on trial or something.

"In a minute," I said, avoiding Wayne's eyes.

The last thing in the world that I wanted was to go and listen to some boring speeches with Wayne, when I could sit here and tell Larry Payne what sort of music I liked.

Wayne gave a kind of a shrug and a skip, and moved off. I knew that he was trying to give the impression that he didn't care if I stayed behind with Larry. Deep inside me, I felt a little pang of guilt. But it was soon swept aside by the tide of excitement as I realised I'd got Larry Payne to myself, on a park bench, in the sunshine. I carefully crossed my legs to try and make my thighs look thinner. They'd been all spread out on the bench, like pillows.

"Music? Well . . . " I dropped my voice and tried to make it husky. "Er, well I like *Rap* — "

Just then Ginger Mike whizzed up. He had borrowed someone's roller-skates and was carrying two hot dogs.

"Ah," he said. "Where's Wayne? Or has he had a head transplant?"

I wanted him to get lost as soon as possible, naturally. The last thing you need, if you're sitting on a bench with Larry Payne, is Ginger Mike hanging around making clever remarks and dripping ketchup all over you.

"He's gone," I said, waving in the direction of the bandstand. "To see the speeches."

"Do you want yours, then?"

Mike waved the horrible greasy smelly hot dog under my nose. Even if it had been the most exquisitely delicious thing ever, I don't think I'd have been able to eat it. My appetite had just vanished. My stomach had been replaced by a sort of dizzy black space with stars. I would probably never eat again.

"No, thanks — ugh. Take it away! I didn't know they were so yukky."

Mike hesitated, rolling from side to side on his skates and looking at us doubtfully.

"Didn't you hear what the lady said?" said Larry suddenly. "Push off, kid."

Mike swooped away immediately. I couldn't believe all this. Larry had called me a *lady*! I hardly dared look at him. I stared across the lake to where the heron had been. But I could feel him looking at my profile, and that made me nervous. If you'd ever seen my profile, you'd know why.

"Fancy coming down the Empire tonight? Bert Broccoli's on."

I could hardly believe my ears. Larry Payne had asked me out! Me! Out! Larry Payne! You get the picture: I was more or less mesmerised. Mustn't seem too keen, though. A scream of joy was dying to burst from my lips, but I pushed it back down past my tonsils and smothered it. It throbbed there for a while and made my ears ring as if I was going to faint.

"Er — tonight?" I husked, twisting one of my hair spikes in what I hoped was a nonchalant manner. "Yeah, why not?"

I'd heard of Bert Broccoli. He was a stand-up comedian and he'd been on the *Late Night TV Show* several times. But I'd have gone like a shot whoever was on. I'd have gone to hear the President of the Women's Institute give a lecture on rice pudding, if Larry Payne had asked me.

Was it really true? Was it all happening? I started to wonder if it was really Larry Payne sitting right next to me, asking me out. Slowly I turned to look at him. And yes, there were those blue eyes, only eighteen inches away, and that black wavy hair, shining in the sun. A great big grin burst over my face. I couldn't stop it.

"That's better," said Larry, and grinned right back at me. So this was it. Life. Love. Happiness. All that. A perfect moment. I felt as if I'd swallowed sunshine.

"Come on," said Larry, getting up and offering me his hand, "let's go and see the action."

I placed my hand in his, and tried to wander nonchalantly along beside him. But it's hard to wander nonchalantly when your heart is transfixed with Life, Love and Happiness. What you really want to do is jump right over the bandstand. I restrained myself, though. I would keep that for later. When we were engaged. When we were married. When our first babies were born. Jet and Samantha — twins.

"Fancy a cup of coffee?" asked Larry.

"Oh yeah, great."

Actually I didn't. I didn't want Larry to see me eat, or drink, ever. Supposing I slurped! Or dribbled all down my sweatshirt! Still, I didn't dare say no in case he thought I was a toffee-nosed git, or a vegetarian, or something. I didn't want to put him off. And I had the terrible feeling that I could do, easily, with the least little thing.

Ginger Mike came swooping past us on his skates. He looked right at our interlinked hands, gave a kind of bow, and called out, "Congratulations" as he flashed by.

"That bloke's a right pill," commented Larry.

I didn't know whether to leap to Ginger Mike's defence, or not. I thought I'd better save it until Larry and I knew each other a little better. I mean, once you know Ginger Mike, you soon find out that he's a terrific guy, even if he is a bit immature and crazy. But I couldn't expect Larry to know that. In fact, looked at objectively, skating around and croaking out his reggae songs with a pair of pink rabbit's ears on his head, Mike did look a bit of a pill. Whatever a pill was. I wasn't sure. But I'm sure it wasn't that bad. I could think of worse names to call somebody.

The main thing was, I was holding Larry's hand!

It was a bit cold, but then, we'd been sitting by the lake, and there'd been a cool breeze blowing.

"Hey, Jane!" I turned. Lorette came striding up. She looked a bit fed up about something. "You seen Wayne?"

I shrugged, hoping to give the impression that whatever else he was, Wayne wasn't my responsibility.

"He went off to listen to the speeches," I said.

The speeches were still booming out over the public address system, and there were big crowds around the bandstand. "He must be somewhere over there."

Lorette didn't look very hard. She was a lot more interested in us. I mean, me and Larry Payne. Get that — us! So we were *us* already. His hand was warming up nicely. I squeezed it shyly, and he nearly broke my knuckles in reply.

"This is Larry Payne," I stammered, realising Lorette didn't really know him. "Do you know Lorette, Larry?"

"Sure," said Larry. "Highfields School's answer to Flo-Jo. Hi."

Lorette nodded. I wished she'd be a bit more forthcoming. But she was so busy trying not to look at us holding hands, she couldn't manage much else. It was a full-time job. I didn't know what was worse, having Ginger Mike staring at our hands, or Lorette discreetly looking everywhere else. Honestly, if I'd known that my hands were going to cause so much interest that day, I'd have washed them a lot more carefully before I came out.

Lorette walked along with us for a while. There were still some stalls I hadn't seen.

"Hey!" said Lorette suddenly, "look at that! What a fantastic idea!"

There in front of us was a stall, a bit like a coconut shy with big pictures pinned up all along the back curtain, of people we love to hate. The Prime Minister, the baddies in certain TV series, and a guy in a bowler hat under which somebody had scrawled The Tax Man. And people were throwing rotten fruit at them. You paid your money and you got two handfuls of rotten apples, oranges, and tomatoes, to throw at the pictures. They were already spattered with juice and pips.

"Well, well, well, look what the dog's brought in!" said a voice. I turned, and there, with a very peculiar look on his face, was Andy Fowler.

"It's brilliant, your stall!" said Lorette.

"It's a nice little earner," he admitted. "A way of making money out of stock that's gone bad." Then he turned to look at the satisfied customers hurling tomatoes at the Prime Minister. He'd seen me and Larry holding hands. That was certain. His grin was subtly different today. A bit defensive.

"Want a go?" he asked.

I was dying to fling a few rotten apples, but Larry pulled me on.

"Nah!" he said. "We got somewhere to go."

Andy Fowler was silent for once. He gave a funny little shrug, threw an apple in the air and headed it away onto the grass.

"I'll have a go," said Lorette, scowling at one of

the pictures. "I'd really like to hit her smack on her stupid snobby stuck-up nose."

"That's what I like — a girl with spirit!" said Andy, but I couldn't hear any more because we were drifting away.

We stopped by the old churchyard and looked back at the fair. I wondered if Larry had forgotten about the coffee.

"Look," he said, "I've got to go. I'm sorry. I just remembered I promised my brother to go up to Edmonton with him to have a look at a bike. So let's leave that coffee till tonight. OK?"

"Fine!"

"I'll meet you — well, by that bus stop outside the chemist's. Passmore's. About eight?"

"OK."

Then he kissed his fingers and tapped me gently on the nose with them. And turned on his heel and went off towards Green Lanes.

5

"You back already?" asked Mum, looking up in surprise from her ironing. Then she must've noticed the excitement streaming off my face because she frowned and peered at me. "What's got into you, Jane?"

"You'll never guess, Mum! Larry Payne asked me out!"

Strangely enough, Mum didn't dance about and toss the ironing in the air in delight. Instead she gave me a not-very-pleasant look.

"And who, may I ask, is Larry Payne?"

"Oh, you know, Mum, he's the school hunk — he's in the sixth form, same as Wayne, and he's really dishy."

Mum looked suspicious.

"How long has this been going on?"

"Going on?" Suddenly I realised that I wasn't exactly on firm ground, here. This had been Going On for about two hours, and if she knew the truth, even my fairly reasonable old mum was going to smell a rat.

"Well, I've sort of, er, known him as a friend for ages," I stammered. "He's — well, he's been around with our gang. Only this is the first time he's, sort of asked me out on my own."

"Where are you going?"

"Oh, not — er, only to the Empire. To see Bert

Broccoli. He's on TV sometimes. You know. You said he was funny, once. Can I go, Mum? Please?"

Mum sighed and started ironing again. She didn't answer. I waited.

"Mum . . . ? Please . . . ?"

"Oh, all right. But you've got to be home by eleven."

"*Eleven?*"

"You heard. Oh, by the way, a parcel came for you."

A parcel? Oh boy. This really was a red-letter day. I grabbed it and tore off the paper. And there, all folded up, was the dark blue silky dress that Wayne had tried to make me buy. I picked it up and held it against myself.

"That's nice, love. Who's it from? Not this Payne whatever his name is?"

"No, no, Mum. It's from — from Lorette and Wayne," I said, blushing. "They were trying to persuade me to get it today, in the park."

"It looks good. Try it on."

I took it to my bedroom. There had been a little card with it, but I hardly dared read it somehow. *Trust me, Jane*, it said in Wayne's funny loopy handwriting. *It'll look great. Call it a late birthday present.*

I flung off my clothes and dived into it. Then I looked at myself in the mirror. I couldn't believe it. It was fantastic. I looked pounds and pounds slimmer, and the way it fluttered round my knees was lovely and tickly. I slipped on a pair of shoes and went to show it to Mum.

"Lovely," she said. "Lorette's got really good taste."

"I'll wear it tonight!" I said. "But first I must have a bath. Is the water hot, Mum?"

I had the longest bath ever, with bubbles right up to my chin like in the old movies. I washed my hair and rinsed it three times, put on too much conditioner and had to rinse it again about six times, until the water ran cold. Mum knocked on the bathroom door.

"Hey!" she called. "Leave a bit of water for the rest of the human race!"

I giggled, but I didn't answer. I had a cucumber and avocado face pack on and I didn't want it to crack.

After the bath, I painted my toenails and finger-nails pale green. Then I decided it looked a bit too weird, and took it all off and put dark pink on instead. Then I decided dark pink was a bit old-fashioned so I took all that off and put some pale green on again. Then I almost fainted because of the smell of the varnish and the remover. I opened my bedroom window and hung out in the fresh air.

The sun was going down over the chestnut trees in the park. The Greenpeace fair was almost over. A couple of swans flew past, their wings making a kind of sawing noise in the air. Something Wayne had said once, came into my head. "They mate for life, swans do."

I leaned my chin on my hands and felt a bit sad and strange and excited all mixed up together. Then I heard the church clock strike and I realised it was nearly time to go. Just a few minutes to check my make-up first.

"What've you got all that green round your eyes for?" asked Mum. "It looks a bit tarty, love."

"Mum! You did the same when you were young! What about the photo of you at that pop festival back in 1972?"

Mum sighed again, and looked at me.

"My little girl, going out on her first date," she said wistfully. I gave her a big hug. I could see she was feeling a bit low. "I hope this Payne person takes good care of you tonight."

"Of course he will, Mum."

"Be back by eleven, then. Have a good time. 'Bye!"

I went.

I tried not to hurry too much as I didn't want to get there first. My blue dress was flapping and dancing around my knees. It felt odd after years of wearing jeans. It made my legs excited. Then suddenly I remembered — I was supposed to meet Lorette and Sudeshna tonight! We'd promised to go to the burger bar where Ginger Mike works on Saturday nights. And I hadn't even told them I couldn't make it! I'd have to drop in at the burger bar, on the way to the Empire, to warn Ginger Mike.

I arrived at the bus stop, and Larry wasn't there. My insides kind of groaned with disappointment. I hesitated. Should I wait here for him, looking as casual and cool as possible? I couldn't bear it, somehow. I was sure everybody would know I was waiting for him. What if he never turned up? I set off round the corner and walked around the block. When I came around the corner again, there he was, standing with his back to me. My heart gave a silly little skip. I walked up behind him and dropped my voice right down to the basement.

"Hello."

He turned round. When he saw my dress, he rolled his eyes and made a funny kind of slurping noise with his lips.

"You look great!" he said.

So, Wayne had been right. I felt grateful and sad and guilty about Wayne all at once. But then Larry Payne grabbed my hand and I forgot about Wayne altogether. We strolled down Church Street. Larry was telling me about the motorbike his brother had bought that afternoon. I tried to listen, but it was hard to concentrate. I kept looking in the shop windows and seeing the two of us reflected together, hand in hand. It didn't really look like me, at all.

Suddenly we were outside the burger bar. This was my chance to leave a message for Lorette and Sudeshna.

"Hey, just a minute," I said. "I ought to leave a message here for my mates."

"Fine," said Larry and we went in. "In fact, why don't we have a bite to eat? I'm starving, and it would save time later."

He led me to a table and we sat down.

I couldn't really argue, but I was in a panic. I didn't want Lorette and Sudeshna to come in and see me here with Larry Payne. I just wanted to leave the message with Ginger Mike and get out. But Larry had other ideas.

Mike came over to us. He looked a bit of an idiot in his cardboard cap.

"Good evening, ladies and gentlemen," he said.

Larry did a double take.

"Oh, you again," he said. "I'd like a quarter pounder with fries and a Coke. How about you, Jane?"

"I — I — er, just some fries, please, Mike. And a Coke."

"Lorette and Sudeshna coming later?" asked Mike, scribbling on his pad.

"Who's Lorette and Sudeshna?" asked Larry. I blushed.

"Oh, just friends of mine. I said I'd meet them here. I mean, originally I said I would. But since we fixed up to go out, I won't be able to. I mean, we'll be gone by the time they come and anyway . . . " I looked at my watch and my voice trailed off. I felt really confused. It was like being in trouble with the headmaster at school. "Can you tell them, Mike? That I'm going to the Empire with Larry tonight?"

"Sure," said Mike. "What Empire is that? The Evil Empire? The Empire Strikes Back?"

"Oh shut up, you idiot!" I snapped. I didn't mean to sound so bitchy. I just wanted Ginger Mike to push off and leave Larry and me alone together. Mike never knows when to keep his mouth shut. He went off to sort out our orders.

"So," said Larry, reaching across the table and squeezing my hands, "here we are. You and me."

"Yeah."

I smiled into his eyes. God, he was gorgeous. I couldn't believe it was fat little me sitting here holding hands with him. Whatever did he see in me? For a moment I was tempted to ask, but then I realised that would be a big mistake. It said so in the magazines. It also said, "When the conversation dries up on your first date, ask him about his interests." So I did.

It was motorbikes again. Personally, I thought we'd already talked enough about motorbikes on the way down Church Street. But Larry seemed to have an endless supply of motorbike stories. He told me about how his brother had done a ton up the M1, and how he'd skidded on ice and nearly got smashed to pieces by an articulated lorry. If I'd been able to concentrate on it, I think I'd have felt quite sick. But I was preoccupied.

Our meal was taking for ever. Mind you, with Ginger Mike in the kitchen, that's no surprise. He made me a cheese sandwich round his house once and it took half an hour. At last, though, he carried two steaming plates to our table — just at the very moment when the door of the burger bar burst open and Lorette and Sudeshna came in — closely followed by Wayne. Luckily Larry had let go of my hands and grabbed his knife and fork. Even so, I felt a huge blush unfold over my face as they came in.

"Hi, gang!" I said in what I hoped was a chirpy confident voice, but which turned out as a loud shriek. "We're just off to the Empire. To see Bert Broccoli."

"Oh really, Jane?" said Sudeshna. "You lucky thing!"

Thank goodness for dear old Sudeshna. Lorette looked even more fed up than she had that afternoon, and Wayne had a smile on his face, but a sad expression hiding in his brown eyes. He looked like a big dog who'd been told off.

"You look great," he said quietly, out of the corner of his mouth, and they sat down at another table. Right. That was over. All I had to do now was eat my chips and drink my Coke.

Easier said than done. I was so anxious to get it over that I burned my tongue on the first chip. So instead of saying, "Really? Fantastic!" whenever Larry paused in his motorbike monologue, all I could manage was, "Leahy? Thandathtic!" I've never found it so hard to eat chips. The pile of them looked immense, like a kind of mountain. I forced down a couple of mouthfuls, and washed it down with a huge swig of Coke. But somehow — you know how it is — I swallowed a huge ball of air with the Coke. I could feel it inching down my throat like a horrible stone or something. It was incredibly painful. And all the time I was nodding and saying, "Leahy? Thandathtic!"

The ball of air reached my stomach, and my stomach wasn't too pleased about it. I knew what was coming now — the most tremendous burp. Oh hell! What could I do? Larry would probably get up and walk straight out if I burped in his face. I knew what I had to do — go to the Ladies and burp there.

"Excuse, me," I muttered, getting up. "Just nip to the loo —"

I was halfway down the aisle towards the loos when the kitchen door swung open and who should come sauntering towards me but . . . Andy Fowler. He'd obviously just delivered some onions or something. I was so amazed to see him, I sort of gasped, and that was it. Out it came — the most deafening burp, right in his face: WAAAAAARP!

"That's the nicest thing you've ever said to me," he grinned, and seized my wrist as I went past. I paused. Andy's hand was strong. He held me still and looked me up and down.

"I'm terribly sorry," I said, apologising to Andy for the first time ever. "It was the Coke."

"You look like a million dollars," he said. "What you doing tonight?"

"I'm going to the Empire," I faltered. "With Larry Payne."

Andy glanced briefly down to where Larry sat.

"Lucky fella," said Andy and let me go. He turned away and sat down with Lorette and the others. I went into the loo.

When I rejoined Larry, he had finished his meal and was picking at my chips.

"Go ahead, finish them," I said. "I'm not very hungry anyway."

"What did that guy say to you?" asked Larry in a low voice.

"Who? Oh — Andy Fowler. Oh, nothing. He's always kidding around."

What was this? Larry Payne jealous — about me? I began to feel good again. This was our first date, and already he was getting all possessive. It was time to get over to the Empire. I knew I'd feel better once we'd left the burger bar. It was kind of distracting, having my mates sitting at the other table. I felt sort of cut in half. Time to go? No. First Larry wanted a coffee.

There was a burst of laughter from the other table. And Fowler was telling a funny story. I could hear odd snatches of it. " . . . Then he said, *I want a straight banana . . .*"

My eyes were drawn over to the other table. Lorette was sitting facing me, listening to Andy. He'd definitely cheered her up. She was smiling all over her face. Well, Andy is a laugh, of course. " . . . And this other old girl came into the shop, and she was really tiny, you know, and my old man said, *Hello, darling' — there's no need to kneel down. We know our fruit's good but there's no need to bleedin' worship it.*"

They all laughed, and I had to try hard to keep the smile off my face, because Larry was deep into a rather tragic story about a motorcycling friend of a friend of his brother's who'd fallen off his Harley-Davidson in Morocco.

"His leg was completely smashed to a pulp," said Larry. "It looked like raw meat . . ."

I was beginning to feel queasy again. I was definitely a vegetarian when it came to conversation. Meanwhile, at the other table, Andy Fowler was unstoppable.

"Lay off, Andy!" Lorette was laughing like a drain. "Or I'll wet myself!"

You don't often hear Lorette say things like that.

She was letting her hair down tonight — metaphorically. Actually it was all plaited and beaded and piled on top of her head. She looked terrific.

"What's the difference between bogies and Brussels sprouts?" Andy was still at it. They all clamoured for him to tell them.

"Well," he said, "you can't get kids to eat Brussels sprouts."

Meanwhile, at our table, Larry was slanging off Arab doctors.

"He was in hospital for twelve weeks, and these guys, they didn't have the first idea. Useless. And sheep's eyeballs for dinner every night."

At Andy's table the talk was more appetising.

"How do you make an apple turnover?"

I didn't hear the answer, because Larry got up to go. At last! I knew our date would start to take off the minute we got away from the gang. As we passed them, they all called out, "Have a great time! Enjoy yourselves!" and for a split second I felt great.

On the bus to the Empire, Larry put his arm round my shoulders, and I snuggled up close to him.

"That Fowler guy, the one with the fruit shop," said Larry. "He used to be at our school, didn't he?"

"Yes. I think he left a couple of years ago."

" 'Sright. He didn't go into the sixth form."

"He went to work in his dad's shop."

"Well, he'd never have made it in the sixth form anyway. Too thick."

I was silent. I didn't think Andy was thick at all.

In fact, his mind seemed too razor-sharp for me. I couldn't keep up.

"Well, he's very funny," I ventured. I didn't want to contradict Larry but I wanted to say something in Andy's favour.

"Huh!" said Larry. "Gets his jokes off the back of a matchbox. Still — don't let's talk about him, eh?"

And he cuddled up to me and we stared into each other's eyes. Our faces were so close I nearly went cross-eyed. His eyes were so big and so blue, it was like looking into a swimming pool.

The show at the Empire was great. Bert Broccoli never mentioned motorbikes once, the *The Dice* were on, and their music always makes me feel happy all over. We walked all the way home, with our arms round each other, and all the way I was thinking, *I wonder if he'll kiss me*, and whether I would know how to do it right, if he did. I've never really been kissed properly, you see. Not by a real boyfriend. I did pretend to kiss Ginger Mike at a party once because everybody else was kissing and nobody wanted to kiss either of us, so we grabbed each other in desperation. But Mike kept his mouth shut and his eyes open all the time and I kept getting the giggles.

My heart beat faster and faster as we went down Ladysmith Road. Thirty more yards, and he might kiss me! But oh help — what if he didn't? What if I'd been so boring and awful, he just wanted to unload me and run off into the night? What if he'd Heard the Burp? I trembled from head to foot.

Thank God it was dark now, so he couldn't see my face. I don't look too bad in the dark.

Suddenly we were there — under the streetlamp. We stopped. I looked up at him and tried to say goodnight in a low husky voice but it came out as a sort of breathless squeak instead. The sort of noise a frightened mouse might make when confronted with a fierce bad lion. Which was, more or less, the situation.

Larry Payne looked down at me for a moment, and then, without saying anything, he grabbed me and sort of bit me on the mouth. It really hurt. Then he stuck his tongue practically down my throat. So this was real kissing. It was more like being eaten alive. All the same, Larry Payne was kissing me goodnight! Larry Payne! Me! Kissing! Once I'd thought of it that way, I started to enjoy the idea. I was sure I'd get used to all the spit and stuff, in time.

I managed to extricate myself after a minute or two, whispered goodnight again and ran off. I wiped my mouth on a tissue as I went up the steps, but I still think I must've looked pretty roughed up when Mum opened the door.

"So," she said curiously. "Have a good time, Jane?"

"Brilliant!" I beamed, and told her all about Bert Broccoli.

I couldn't sleep for hours. I lay in bed turning everything over in my mind. I wondered if I was in love. I was sure I was. After all — Larry Payne! I was thinking about him so hard, there wasn't room in my mind for anything else. I didn't dream about him, though. When I finally drifted off to sleep. I had a nightmare. I was drowning in a swimming pool and then suddenly all the water ran away down a sort of giant plughole, and I was almost sucked down it. Then I looked up and I could see Lorette and Wayne and the gang all looking down into this deep dark pit, and I was in the bottom of it, and I couldn't — oh sorry. I'd forgotten how boring it is, listening to people's dreams.

6

On the bus on Monday morning, Lorette was odd. I was bursting to tell her all about my date with Larry, but she wasn't in a very good mood.

"Everything's gone wrong this morning!" she grumbled. "My dad yelled at me. The yoghurt had gone off an' all. Got me off to a real bad start."

"Oh," I said. "Well, never mind. We can buy you something at Peck's when we get off the bus."

"I don't want any of that crap they got in there!" she snapped. "All those chocolate bars and stuff. Crammed with additives."

"I think they have — well, muesli bars," I suggested.

"I hate them! They're so sticky, it makes my teeth ache just lookin' at them."

Lorette stared out gloomily at Newington Green. I hesitated.

"Don't you want to hear about my date with Larry?" I asked at last. Lorette turned and looked me straight in the eye. Not in a very friendly way, either.

"That was all very sudden," she said sharply. "You don't believe in hangin' about, do you?"

"Well, it wasn't me," I stammered. "It was him. I mean, he's very — like — impulsive."

I liked the word *impulsive*. It made Larry sound like the hero of a real love story.

"I thought he was re-pulsive, myself."

I was terribly hurt.

"Lorette! Don't say that! I went out with him! He's great!"

"Tell me what's so great about him, then."

I'd really chosen the wrong moment to talk about this.

"Well, he's, well, incredibly dishy . . . I mean — "

"I know what he looks like, Jane. I've seen quite enough of him. He's not my type, thanks very much."

"No, well, it's a good job, too, isn't it? I mean, I wouldn't like us to split up over a boy."

I gave a hollow laugh.

"Look, Jane," Lorette fixed me with a stern glare. "I really care about you, right? You're my best mate. But I'm worried about you now. I mean, what's this guy like deep down inside?"

"Well, I don't know yet," I admitted. "I haven't really had a chance to get to know him, well, properly."

"What's he interested in?"

"Motorbikes." I tried to make it sound fascinating, but Lorette only sort of snorted.

"Motorbikes! Typical. Aggro-machines. An' they pollute the environment and all, with their horrible noise and burnin' of carbon monoxide."

I was silenced. I had to admit I've never been a bike freak.

"I'm sorry I didn't have a chance to warn you that I couldn't come out with you guys on Saturday night."

Lorette tossed her head.

" 'Sall right. We had a great time anyway."

"Good. That Andy Fowler is a real laugh, isn't he?"

Lorette smiled for the first time that morning. Thank God for Andy Fowler. Then she told me all the funny things he had done and said, and by the time we got off the bus, we were helpless with laughter and other people on the bus were beginning to give us snooty stares.

As we walked past the sixth-form block, I noticed Larry leaning against one of the pillars. He gave me a special wink. I tried to wink back, but my eyelid sort of seized up so I just grinned and blushed instead. Then I noticed Wayne, hanging about a bit further away. For the first time, he turned away without even a grin, and started doing some standing press-ups against the wall.

I decided I'd better not mention Larry Payne to Lorette again. At least not until she'd had a chance to get to know him better. I knew what I'd have to do — I'd give a kind of little party at my house so everybody could meet him properly. Yes! That'd be great. I must ask Mum as soon as I got home. Then Mum could meet him as well. It was a shame nobody in our gang really knew him. Except Wayne. And Wayne had never said much — except to tease me. He didn't look in the mood for teasing today.

I had to tell somebody how marvellous it all was. Ginger Mike ought to be aware of the inter-galactic wonderfulness of it all. I cornered him at break.

"I had a fantastic date with Larry on Saturday, Mike."

"Oh yeah?"

Mike was fiddling with his pen, putting a refill in. He didn't look up.

"That meal you got us was delicious."

"You left yours."

"Er — well, that was because I wasn't hungry. I was, sort of too excited as well."

Ginger Mike looked round the room and whistled quietly. He didn't seem to be listening. He didn't seem to want to know about me being excited.

"And Bert Broccoli was terrific."

"Yeah! He's great!" Mike seized the subject. "I saw him once on the *Late Night TV Show* and he did this amazing thing with his face — he sort of folded it in half and made it into a guided missile."

"It was brilliant seeing him in person. It was a great way to spend my first date."

Mike looked back at his pen, and started unscrewing it. Suddenly I realised that he was too immature and uncertain about life to talk about — well, relationships and things like that. Dates. Boy meets girl. Dear old Mike. He just couldn't take it. Too embarrassed. I pulled his hair affectionately and went off to look for Sudeshna.

I found her in the cloakrooms ransacking her locker. She immediately offered me about three thousand calories in a chewy bar the size of a matchbox. I said no. The funny thing was, since I'd got going with Larry, I hardly felt like eating much at all.

"Hey, Sudeshna," I whispered. "Want to hear about my date with Larry Payne?"

Sudeshna giggled and we sat down together. This was more like it.

"He's really sensational, Sudeshna. It was fantastic!" Sudeshna giggled again.

"How late did you stay out?"

"Oh, only till eleven."

Sudeshna's eyes widened.

"*Eleven*?" Poor old Sudeshna. She has to be in by nine — when she's allowed out at all. "What was he like, Jane?"

"Oh, ever so nice. He was, well — sort of shy."

Yes. That was probably it. That was why I realised I hadn't got much idea of what Larry was like, yet. He was definitely shy.

"*Shy*? I didn't think he was like that. I thought he was, well — quite proud."

"Proud?" I panicked slightly. I knew what she meant. He did give the impression of being a bit, well . . . but when you got to know him, you realised right away that it was just that he was shy. I explained all this to Sudeshna and she nodded seriously. Then she said,

"What did your mum say?"

"What did my *mum* say?"

What a crazy question. I ask you.

"Oh, she was fine," I said. "She was pleased for me."

"Really?" Sudeshna sighed. "My parents would kill me if I went out with a boy, like that."

"What do you mean, like that?"

"Well, just from meeting him in the park."

I felt a bit anxious.

"How are you supposed to meet boys, then?"

"Well, I think it's different for me. Because I wouldn't dream of going out with a boy, you see, Jane. I couldn't even think of it."

Poor Sudeshna. No wonder she kept gobbling up all those chocolate bars.

"But how — but why can't you — ?"

"My parents want me to have an arranged marriage."

"Arranged?" It sounded awful. "But he could be old, or fat. What if you don't like him?"

Sudeshna giggled again.

"Well, your romantic sort of marriages don't last very well, do they? How many people get divorced is it? A third?"

She was right, there. My mum and dad, for a start.

"But surely you wouldn't want your family to choose a husband for you, when you could choose one for yourself?"

"I don't know. My parents' marriage was arranged. And they're quite happy together. And I think I know who they might be thinking of."

"What — for you?"

"Yes. His dad's a friend of my uncle's. Back home."

"Have you ever met him?"

"Not since I was little," Sudeshna giggled again. "But I've got a photograph."

"What's he look like? Can I see it?"

Shyly Sudeshna opened her wallet, then showed me a photo of a guy with jet black hair and smouldering eyes. He was a hunk of truly mouthwatering quality. I boggled.

"Crumbs, Sudeshna! Why didn't you ever show me this before? He's fantastic!"

Then Sudeshna got a really fatal case of giggling and whipped her wallet away again.

"Well! If he's got any spare brothers lying around, tell your dad he can arrange a marriage for me, too!" I said. Sudeshna suddenly screamed and got a coughing fit. She was just smothering herself with her scarf, when the bell rang.

I didn't feel that Sudeshna really approved of me going out with Larry Payne. I was beginning to feel a bit guilty, myself. But no! Why should I feel like that? It was great, it was the most exciting thing that had ever happened to me. What a shame I couldn't talk about it properly with my mates.

At lunchtime I went off by myself and leant on a wall looking over the tennis courts. I knew Larry was busy doing his weight training and I wouldn't see him, so if I couldn't see him, and I couldn't talk about him, I wanted to be alone to dream about him. Just then somebody walked up next to me and leant on the wall too.

"Hi, Jane."

It was Wayne. Suddenly I felt speechless. But there were some things I just had to say.

"That dress you gave me is really wonderful, Wayne."

"Yeah. You looked great in it. I told you."

"I'll always trust your taste in future."

"Will you?" He gave me a funny look. Silence fell. Then my feelings burst out. They had to.

"Oh Wayne! I'm really sorry I had to go off on Saturday. I mean — "

"I know what you mean, sister. Relax."

"But I just — "

"Yeah. Cool it. You couldn't help yourself."

"He's so fantastic, Wayne!"

"He's a good-lookin' guy."

Wayne was crumbling up the edge of the wall, and looking at the people playing tennis. But I felt extremely close to him, much closer than I had to anybody all morning.

"You understand me, Wayne."

"I worry about you, too, Jane."

"There's no need to worry about me."

"You sure?"

He turned and gave me a very serious, searching look.

"Absolutely."

" 'Cos if anybody hurts you, ever, I'm gonna kick his head right off."

"No need. I've had my first self-defence classes, remember?"

"Oh yeah. How's it going?"

I began to tell him about it, but neither of us was really interested. We had other things on our minds. I broke off.

"Wayne — "

"What?"

"I feel, I mean, I really ought to apologise to you. Somehow."

"No need, sister. No need."

"But the way I went off with Larry on Saturday. And I wore your dress to — to go out with him."

"Listen, Jane. That was not my dress. That was your dress. You don't worry about a thing, now.

I'm your friend. Remember that. That's what I want to be. Your friend and your bodyguard."

For a minute I felt like giving him a big hug, but I thought the better of it and punched him in the stomach instead. Then we did a little wrestling. He said he wanted to test my self-defence progress. I wasn't much good at it yet, though. I noticed how terrifically strong Wayne was. I was glad he was my friend and bodyguard. It was the nicest thing anyone had said to me for ages.

And it made me feel somehow better all over. We were still wrestling when Lorette ran up. A silly grin was plastered all over her face.

"Listen!" she said. "Guess what! Mrs Andrews has just told me I got selected to go for the International Under 18 trials next month."

Wayne was so amazed, he threw me into the air and I yelled like a banshee. Then Mrs Fisher came over and told us to cut it out. But when we told her that Lorette was going to be a big shot international star, she was so pleased, she managed a whole smile, with both sides of her face, for the first time that term. This was it. Definitely. The start of the big time.

7

Mum seemed quite keen on the idea of a little party at our place: just Larry Payne and my mates and her. I bet she was dying of curiosity. Once I started to plan it, though, I sort of panicked. Mum insisted it had to be in the daytime as she needs her beauty sleep. She's right about that, actually. Whenever she's had a late night, she gets such big bags under her eyes, she practically needs a trolley to carry them into the bathroom.

"Whatever shall we have to eat?"

I wouldn't have worried, somehow, if it was just my mates, but the thought of Larry being there made me feel really tense.

"How about pizza?" asked Mum.

"Brilliant!"

"Tell you what, then — you do the shopping, and buy a lettuce too, and then I'll make the pizza if you make the salad."

"Great! Thanks, Mum! You're terrific!"

Mum wrote out the shopping list whilst I put my trainers on. My jeans were beginning to feel baggy. I hadn't been eating nearly so much recently and I must've lost quite a lot of weight. In fact, that morning when I'd pulled my jeans on and stood up, they'd nearly fallen down again, and I'd had to keep them up with a belt. I was really pleased. Larry was having a good effect, all round. I just hoped Mum would like him.

I nipped off up the road with the shopping basket, and then started to read the list. Lettuce, onions, olives, tomatoes, celery . . . I was definitely going to have to go into Fowler's. I hoped that Andy's dad would be there. Somehow I felt a bit embarrassed about seeing Andy. I had a feeling he might tease me about Larry. I wasn't going to be able to avoid him, though. There he was, serving an old lady. I opened the door and crept in.

When she'd gone out, Andy turned to me with a rather pale sort of smile.

"Hi!" he said. "What can I get you?"

This was so unlike the way he'd always talked to me, kidding me along, throwing things at me, hanging cherries from my ears, that I suddenly felt quite cold inside.

"Er — a pound of tomatoes, please, Andy." I buried my face in the shopping list. He weighed out the tomatoes in silence, and put them in my basket. Then he looked closely at my face.

"You look a bit peaky," he said. "Been ill?"

"No — just lost a bit of weight. You should be glad. You always said I was too fat!"

The words came spilling out before I could stop them. Andy looked puzzled.

"What the hell you on about?" he asked. "You round the bend or something? I never said any such thing."

He sounded quite cold, and angry. I started to tremble.

"Oh, sorry, then," I tried to sound proud and scornful. "It must've been somebody else."

"Yeah. It must've."

"Er — a lettuce, please."

I went on right down the list, and Andy got the things and put them in the basket. Neither of us said anything. I longed for his dad to come and make a joke or two. He sometimes sends something home for my mum — seed potatoes, that sort of thing. They know each other because they've both got allotments. But he didn't appear.

"Right, then," I said, "that's all."

Andy totted up the price on the till, and I fumbled in my purse for the money. It seemed to take ages to find it, but at last I cornered it and put it in his hand. His hand seemed very big, and felt very warm, as it brushed against my finger tips. I stood still for a moment, wanting to say something but not able to find any words.

"It wouldn't have been me," he said, finally, turning back from the till. "I liked you fine as you were."

There was something in his eyes that I couldn't bear.

Just then a little old lady came in, and he broke into a dazzling grin for her, as if she was his most favourite person in the whole world and I was the biggest turn-off. I slunk out.

I did the rest of Mum's shopping, feeling sick. It was as if somebody was pulling my stomach down, down into the earth. I tried to shake it off, to think of other things, but my mind seemed horribly hypnotised by that episode in the fruit shop. Tears kept welling up behind my eyes but I squeezed them back into my head. I wasn't having any of that rubbish. It was my party today!

For a split second I thought of going back to the fruit shop and inviting Andy. Then I realised that he was the last person I wanted to be there. I concentrated hard on the plan. Larry was going to arrive early, in time for a little chat with Mum, and the others were coming at one. Mum would have to get cracking with her pizzas. I turned the corner and was just about to run home when I bumped into Ginger Mike coming out of the chemist's.

"Just picked up a new prescription for my mum," he whispered. "Really far-out stuff. I'll bring some to your party."

"Don't you dare, you idiot!" I yelled. "My mum'll be there, and I don't want anything to do with that kind of horrible bloody rubbish!"

And I gave him a terrific clout on the shoulder with a stick of celery. Ginger Mike looked surprised.

"Nothing like a party to cheer you up," he observed, and slipped past me.

"Come at one!" I called after him. "Don't be late!"

I desperately needed Ginger Mike to be there. He's great for cheering things up. Sometimes I think he ought to be on hire, for getting parties going. Also the way he dances makes everyone crack up. Not that there was going to be any dancing at my party. It was going to be terribly civilised and grown-up.

I crossed the road so I wouldn't have to pass by Fowler's Fruit Shop, and ran all the way home. It was getting easier to run, now I was thinner. I liked the feeling. But was I really looking peaky? As soon as I got in, I dumped the shopping on the kitchen table and ran into the bathroom to take a peek in the mirror. My face did look thinner. I liked it. But there was a funny anxious look in my eyes. Ah well. A bit of mascara would soon take care of that.

Larry was late. Everything was ready, and I'd got enough mascara on my eyelashes to keep a locomotive running smoothly — that's what Mum said, anyway. She was sitting knitting. I couldn't sit still. My heart was thundering away as if it would split my ribs. What if he didn't come? What would Mum think? How could I ever look my friends in the face? And how on earth was I going to manage to eat even a tiny little piece of pizza?

The front doorbell rang. I kind of lurched out to answer it and banged my hand on the doorpost. Then I had to pretend I wasn't on tenterhooks as I opened the door. I madly tried to pull on an expression of casual, carefree oh-hello-it's-you, like a sort of invisible pullover. But it got stuck over my ears.

"Lerro Harry!" I gasped.

This was not a good start. This was slightly less than the great vamps of the past would've managed. He grinned and came in. I could see he was thinking about whether to kiss me or not, so I nipped out of the way double-quick and ran into the sitting room.

"Come in!" I called out. "Mum, this is Larry Payne. Larry, this is my mum."

They shook hands. He smiled at her. She smiled at him. So far so good! It was going all right!

"Hello, Mrs Watts," said Larry. "Nice to meet you."

Mum asked him to sit down and got him a Coke. I had a Coke too, and I tried to take a sip to steady my nerves. Instead a bubble went soaring up the back of my throat and made me hiccup. I should know better by now. When I'm in a jam, Coke always lets me down.

"So. I've heard a lot about you, Larry," said Mum. "Where do you live?"

They talked about where Larry lived for a while, but I couldn't concentrate. I kept looking at his clothes and wondering if Mum liked them. He was wearing a navy sweatshirt and jeans and very white trainers. He looked fine. Fine? He looked gorgeous. But I didn't dare think about how gorgeous he looked — not with Mum right there in the very same room.

"What are you thinking of doing after school?" asked Mum, with her head cocked on one side. She always does that when she's trying to make up her mind about something.

"Well, I'm hoping to go to university," said Larry. That sounded terrific. I was sure she'd go for that. It made Larry seem very important.

"I've applied to Leeds to read Engineering," he said.

Leeds! That was miles away, wasn't it — up north somewhere? Suddenly the thought hit me that Larry would be going right away for weeks on end. Still, it wasn't until the year after next. By then we might be — but I didn't let myself complete that thought. The future had become difficult, and exciting, and too bright to look at.

"Engineering? That sounds like a good idea," said Mum. "You could work anywhere in the world, then."

"I fancy the Middle East," said Larry.

I didn't. It sounded hot and dangerous. But Larry seemed to know exactly what he wanted, what sort of future he was headed for. I wondered if I'd feel the same when I was seventeen.

"That's where the big money is, I reckon," he said. Mum was watching him with a strange expression on her face. Big money isn't really something we're used to in our house. We tend to live on the other sort — small money. So small, sometimes, it tends to disappear down the cracks between the floorboards.

"Get a big contract with one of these oil sheiks," Larry went on. He sounded like a proper grown-up man. I hoped Mum was impressed. "Well, you're made, aren't you? Dubai, that's where the money is. They're loaded. They paper the walls with it, out there."

"So that's your main ambition, is it, Larry?" asked Mum, pouring him more Coke.

"Yeah!" he grinned. "I want to travel and this way I can go places and make a packet, too. Mind you, I don't fancy some of these Far East countries. The Pakis are welcome to it. And it's welcome to them."

"Don't you have any Asian friends?" asked Mum.

"Nah. There's Imtiaz at school, but he's a bit of a pillock. They're all pillocks if you ask me. Well . . . I suppose Imran Khan's all right."

I was beginning to wish Larry would talk about something else, when the doorbell rang. I ran to answer it and there were Lorette and Wayne and Mike and Sudeshna. They all came in and made a noise and suddenly the house seemed full. They'd brought things too: Sudeshna had brought a big box of chocolates and Lorette had got a lovely bunch of flowers for my mum.

"Oh thanks, Lorette!" she said, beaming. I was so proud of Lorette for thinking of it. Dear old Mum. I should remember to get her flowers myself, sometimes. "How kind. You are a thoughtful girl!" And she ran off to put them in water.

"Hi, Larry," said Wayne, sitting down next to him. "How's tricks?"

"All right, mate," said Larry. "My brother's got that old Norton I was telling you about."

I offered them all drinks and ran about in a flap. After Larry had finished talking about his brother's motorbike, there was a short silence. I felt awful.

"Jane was telling me you've been selected for the international team, Lorette," said Mum quickly.

"Yeah," said Lorette. "Well, the trials, anyway. It's at White City on the sixteenth. They're choosing the British Under 18 team."

"I'm sure you'll do well," said Mum. "You deserve to."

"I'm her coach," said Ginger Mike. "We're going to be training hard for the next two weeks. I'm flying her down to the Australian desert and

81

she's going to run over sand dunes dressed in a plastic bag for six hours a day."

We all laughed. Even Larry smiled. It was funny, sitting next to Wayne he looked smaller and paler and his trainers were somehow rather too white. I expect they were new. Perhaps he'd even bought them in my honour! No, that was silly. Of course he hadn't.

Then Lorette started to tell us about her real training with Mrs Andrews. I was so excited about the thought of Lorette getting selected and flying off to compete in foreign countries, I even sort of forgot about Larry for a minute. But then I realised, gradually, that he hadn't said anything for a while. I wished he would. I wished he would say what a good runner Lorette was, how hard she trained, or something. But he didn't. I wished he'd say something quite ordinary like, "Where do you get your running shoes from?" But he didn't even say that.

"Let's have some lunch!" said Mum eventually. The pizza was sizzling away under the grill and the smell was delicious. Mum's pizzas really are ace. The trouble was, my stomach was churning and churning with nerves and I wasn't sure I'd be able to eat even a mouthful.

We all sat round the table — it was crowded and nice, like a real party. I was sitting with my back to the window, opposite Larry. Our eyes met for a split second and I gave him the most dazzling grin. I couldn't help it. I felt so happy that he was here, having lunch with me and my mum and my mates. I expect he would start talking to them, any minute. He didn't exactly grin back, just gave a little sort of smile and turned to look at the food. I expect he was shy. How sweet!

Ginger Mike took a huge bite out of his pizza and started chewing it. His jaws kind of crack when he chews. Sudeshna nibbled hers. Lorette was sucking her fingers where she'd got salad dressing on them. Lucky old Lorette can eat loads and never gets fat because she takes so much exercise. Mind you, by now I wasn't really fat either. It was all this excitement. I knew I couldn't eat. I cut my pizza into three bits and then into six. Then I moved the bits round my plate.

The others were talking about pizzas. Wayne said this was the best pizza he'd ever had, and Mum blushed and looked pleased, and then Lorette remembered a terrible pizza they'd had when they went to Southend for the day. Ginger Mike said he was sure he'd had a worse pizza in Brighton. Sudeshna giggled quietly and looked happy. I put a pice of pizza in my mouth. It felt odd. I chewed it, and the more I chewed it, the bigger and drier it seemed to become.

If only Larry would say something. He had finished his pizza and now he was staring out of the window. Lorette was talking, but he wasn't looking at her. I wished he would. I looked at her very hard, to try and set him an example, but I could tell out of the corner of my eye that he still wasn't paying attention. Wayne made a joke, and everybody laughed. When Larry heard them laughing he sort of woke up and joined in, but I could tell he hadn't really been listening.

"What about you, Larry?" asked Mum. "Have you ever had a really awful meal?"

Clever Mum. She could tell he was shy. Maybe he felt awkward because we were all fourth formers — except Wayne. But Mum would make him feel at ease.

"Yeah," said Larry. "I went and had an Indian meal once. Curry, you know. Down that place on the corner of Pilkington Street. Made me ill for a week."

"Oh dear!" said Mum. "Well, there's a lot of food poisoning about, these days."

"Yeah. Specially in these Indian joints." When he said that, Sudeshna went quiet and sat very still and looked at her plate. "God knows what was in that curry. Somebody's pussy cat, probably."

"Well, curry's my favourite," said Wayne. "You can get food poisoning just as easy from a British Rail sandwich."

"Easier!" added Lorette. "Because the curry's sort of, like an antibiotic, see? And you get lots of onion and garlic with it, that's a natural antibiotic too, right? So Indian food's safer than English if it's cooked properly. Better for you an' all."

There was another silence. Then Mum collected up the plates. Sudeshna gave a grateful little look at Wayne and Lorette. I felt completely tongue-tied. A peculiar feeling was welling up inside me, like a giant football. I pushed it down, and tried to listen to Wayne and Ginger Mike talking about the film they were going to that night. I was due to go out with Larry, but they were going to see the new John Cleese film. I felt a bit jealous really. I love

John Cleese. But of course I'd rather be going out with Larry.

He stood up, suddenly, and gave my mum a sort of nod and a smile.

"Thanks very much for the lunch, Mrs Watts," he said. "I must be off."

"Right, Larry," said Mum, wiping her hands. "It was very nice to meet you."

It was all a bit stiff and awkward. Larry moved towards the door. I followed to see him out. He turned to the others.

"Cheers," he said. They all looked a bit doubtful and Sudeshna looked scared, but Wayne was relaxed. He waved.

"See you, mate," he said.

I saw Larry out. He paused by the door, and whispered, "See you tonight by the bus stop at eight?"

I nodded. He blew me a kiss, and was gone.

The others didn't stay very long after that. But even I could tell that the minute Larry was gone, everything relaxed. We could all feel it. There was a lot of giggling and fooling around. But nobody mentioned Larry. There was a kind of deafening silence on the subject. And the odd football feeling inside me wouldn't go away.

After the gang had gone, I helped Mum wash up. I felt strange and uneasy even with her. I was dying to ask her what she thought of Larry but somehow I didn't dare. We hardly talked at all, in fact. I put the radio on to hide the silence. It was Mum's favourite Saturday afternoon jazz. But as she finished the drying-up she gave a deep sort of sigh.

"I hope you know what you're doing, Jane, love," she said.

I backed away towards the stairs.

"Oh yes, well, I'm, you know, I'm not stupid, Mum."

Mum looked at me with a sad sort of expression on her face.

"He wasn't very nice to Sudeshna."

"He didn't mean it! It sort of came out all wrong. I think he's a bit shy."

Mum turned away and got out her gardening gloves.

"I'm going down the allotment," she said. "I need a good dig."

After she'd gone, I went into my bedroom, lay down on the bed and wrapped a pillow round my head. Then I screamed into it for about two minutes. When I got up again I felt better. At least I was seeing Larry again tonight. Twice in one day! I went to make myself a piece of toast. I was feeling all hollow and empty, and I knew in a couple of hours I'd start feeling too nervous to eat, again. It was hard work, having a love life. It was a full-time job.

8

When Mum got back from the allotments there was a funny smile on her face. She sang as she put the kettle on, and she didn't bother to sniff the milk suspiciously as she usually does, before putting it in our tea.

"Turnips coming on all right then, Mum?" I asked. I haven't a clue about gardening. It seems dead boring to me. If I had to go off on a Saturday afternoon and dig and weed for a couple of hours, I think I'd go round the bend. But here she was grinning and humming to herself as if she was on top of the world. It must be really weird, being middle-aged.

"We don't grow turnips, Jane," she reminded me. "You don't like them. You say they smell like dirty socks — remember?" Then she got up suddenly and went to look in the mirror.

"Do you think I should wash my hair?" she asked.

"No. It's fine."

Mum's hair is really good — strong and black and wavy. Too bad I inherited Dad's — limp and thin and gerbil brown. It takes me an hour with the gel and the hairdrier to persuade it to defy gravity.

"I think I will, all the same."

And off she went to the bathroom and washed

her hair — right in the middle of her cup of tea. I don't mean she actually *washed her hair in tea*, but — oh, forget it.

Afterwards she came in towelling it and gave me a really friendly grin.

"Going anywhere nice tonight, Jane?"

"Oh, down the Empire I think. Larry likes it down there."

"He's very good-looking, love."

"Do you think so, Mum? Oh great!"

This was the first word of approval. I was really chuffed.

"Watch out for him, though, Jane. Handsome is as handsome does."

Then she dried her hair. It was more or less time for me to get ready for my date. I got up. It's a long job, trying to disguise Jane Watts as a dishy young girl-about-town. It was going to take skill, imagination and a hell of a lot of make-up.

As I walked out, Mum switched off the hairdrier and called out, in a funny kind of voice,

"Jane . . . ?"

"What, Mum?"

"I'll . . . I'll . . . "

She hesitated. This was odd. Was she going to say something else about Larry? Good or bad? My heart beat a little faster. I did so want her to like him.

"Jane, I'm . . . well, I'm going out myself this evening."

"What, to see Auntie Fran? OK."

"No, not Fran. I'm — I'm going out, Jane, with Tony Fowler."

My mind went blank. Tony Fowler? The name was sort of familiar.

"Who?"

"Andy Fowler's dad. You know, from the fruit shop!"

I was amazed. Mum was going out on a date! With Andy Fowler's dad! Mrs Fowler had run off with a double-glazing salesman, yonks ago — Tony Fowler and Mum were both single parents. Mum looked up at me, a bit uncertainly, and I realised she was embarrassed. And shy! And wanted me not to be upset!

"I — I hope you don't mind, Jane."

"*Mind*? You silly old thing, Mum! It's great! You should've done this long ago."

And I bounded across the room and gave her a great big hug.

"Really? Are you sure?"

" 'Course you should. I've been worried about you for ages. I've wanted you to. You should've done it before."

"Well," said Mum with a silly grin, "he didn't ask me till today."

"I hope you have a really brilliant time. Where are you going?"

"To have a curry. Then maybe to a film. Make sure you've got your key, Jane."

Mum looked really happy. I gave her a smacking kiss and then ran off to start on my eyes.

Andy Fowler's dad is quite a comedian — like his son. He looks a bit like that actor, John Hurt. He's got a sort of thin craggy face, and I knew Mum would have really good fun with him. I wondered if they would fall in love. Do people fall in love when they're forty? It's odd to think of it. I was glad he wasn't the fat slob kind of middle-aged man. Ugh! Really cringe-making.

Mum looked fantastic for her date. She'd made a real effort. She looks good in turquoise and black, and she'd taken her jeans and trainers off for once and got her black skirt and party shoes on. She looked uncertain, though.

"Do I look OK, Jane?" she asked. It was strange for a minute — as if she was my sister or something.

"You look sensational," I said and hugged her. It's great, having a young mum. Mike's mum is about fifty-five or something. "I was a late baby," Ginger Mike told me once. "That's why I'm such very very high quality."

As I walked up the road, leaving Mum combing her hair in the bathroom mirror for the nineteenth time, I met Andy Fowler's dad walking down past the pub.

"Hello, darlin'!" he said with a grin. "That mum of yours ready for a great night out?"

"You bet! Take care of her," I said. "Tell her how gorgeous she looks."

"No problem. Hey! You and Andy should get together and come out with us one day. Have a foursome."

Something inside me exploded, and a truly enormous blush rushed down from my hair to my toes. It was so powerful, I was surprised the pavement didn't turn pink.

"I'm — well, I'm going out with Larry Payne, at the moment, actually."

"Oh — right — good for you, love. Sorry I spoke. Have fun then."

And he was off.

It took me a long time to recover from that thought. Andy and me getting together. I was trembling all over, and my knees had gone sort of weak. I don't know why. Embarrassment, I suppose. I had to pull myself together before Larry turned up, so I tried to think of other things. Like Lorette being chosen to run for the British Under 18 Athletics team.

Just as I turned the corner into Church Street, I saw Sudeshna coming out of her shop. She was crying. I ran up.

"Sudeshna? What's wrong?" I asked.

"It's my dad. He got beaten up. Some men came in and took the money from the till. They hit him on the head when he tried to stop them."

"What — now? Just now?"

"An hour ago. The ambulance came to take him to hospital. He said he was all right but they told him he should have an X-ray just to make sure." Sudeshna wiped her eyes, and blew her nose.

"Is your mum OK?"

"Yes. She just sent me along to Mrs Patel's to ask Mr Patel if he could help to clear up the mess and put a new window pane in. They broke a pane of glass."

"Can I help?"

"Oh, thanks, Jane; but I don't think so. Maybe just say hello to my mum." Sudeshna went off to the Patels', and I went into the shop. There was glass all over the floor, and Mrs Chakravarti was picking it up carefully and putting it in a dustpan.

"Mrs Chakravarti! I'm so sorry. Sudeshna just told me what happened. Is there anything I can do?"

"No thanks, Jane. We've had the police and my husband's gone off for his X-ray — Mr Patel will mend the window."

"Who were they?"

"My husband said two West Indian boys and a white boy. Never seen them before. From Tottenham or somewhere." She sighed, and sat down by the till. She looked tired. There were shadows round her big brown eyes. She must've been as beautiful as Sudeshna, once.

"Not enough discipline," said Mrs Chakravarti, smoothing her shiny black hair down as if to comfort herself. "Not enough control in the family." She shook her head.

It seemed horrendous that a nice gentle family like the Chakravartis, who've never done any harm to anyone, should be attacked like this. They stay open late so people can shop after six. And they work incredibly hard. I felt furious, but there really didn't seem anything I could do.

By the time Sudeshna came back, she looked a bit calmer. Mr Patel arrived with his toolbox and it seemed to be time I left. So I just said again that if there was anything Mum or I could do, they should ring, and I stepped outside.

There, across the street at the bus stop, stood Larry Payne. I'd completely forgotten I was on my way to a date with him. So many distracting and dramatic things seemed to be happening today. I nipped across the road, and grabbed his hand. I wanted to tell him all about the robbery, but he got in first, and there was something not-quite-totally pleased about the way he looked at me.

"You're late," he said.

9

We went to another hamburger joint. Not Ginger
Mike's, thank goodness. I didn't want a repeat of
the last time.

"Let's go down the High Street instead," said
Larry. "That Mike bloke gets on my wick."

I didn't argue. I know Mike's a bit strange, and
it always takes people a while to get used to his
jokes and his funny ways. Once Larry got to know
him really well, he'd think he was great, I was sure.

"So," said Larry, as we sat down and got stuck
into our milkshakes, "what kept you?"

I told him all about the attack on Sudeshna's
dad.

"It was these young blokes," I said. "They
bashed him on the head and took the money out
of the till. He had to go to hospital and have an
X-ray. Isn't it awful!"

"I wish I'd been there," said Larry. "I'd have
had a go at the bastards." He flexed his fists and
glowered across the table at me. It was quite
impressive.

"There were three of them," I said. "Poor Mr
Chakravarti didn't stand a chance."

"What were they?" asked Larry. "Black?"

"Two black guys and a white one."

"Typical." Larry picked up a plastic cup and
crushed it to bits in his fist. I wasn't sure what he

meant by *typical*. But somehow I was too scared to ask.

"It's a shame Mr Chakravarti hasn't got someone like you as his bodyguard," I said instead.

"Yeah. I'd have sorted them out. You'd have needed a trowel to get 'em off the pavement."

This was a rather horrible thought somehow. But I was grateful that Larry felt so strongly about what had happened to poor Sudeshna and her family.

"They stole a whole day's takings," I told him.

"Well, I don't suppose old Chakravarti will notice that," said Larry, cracking each of his knuckles in turn as if getting them into training. He looked as if he was just dying to punch someone's teeth down their throat. "They make a bomb, these Asian guys," he went on.

"Oh I don't think so — but anyway, even if they do, they deserve it. The shop's open from seven-thirty in the morning till ten at night. Honestly! Not many people would be willing to work those hours."

"The trouble is," Larry looked out of the window at the lorries thundering up the High Street, "the guy's such a wimp."

"What? Who?"

"Chakravarti. He's such a little guy. Shoulders like a coat hanger. Like something off an Oxfam poster."

"What's that got to do with it?" I couldn't understand what Larry meant.

"Well, look at it from these guys' point of view. He was asking for it."

"What?" I couldn't believe my ears.

"A little puny guy like that, all alone in his shop all evening."

I couldn't think what to say. It sounded as if Larry was making excuses for the robbers. As if he thought it was somehow Mr Chakravarti's fault. As if being small and weak and gentle meant you were asking for trouble and got what you deserved. I started biting my nails, then suddenly realised what I was doing and stopped. It had taken me six months' intensive effort to stop biting them. And here I was undoing all the hard work in three minutes.

Larry suddenly turned away from the window and seemed to notice that I wasn't looking too happy.

"Not that that's any excuse," he said, and grabbed my hand. "I just wish I could've had a crack at the bastards."

Then he smiled and squeezed my hand, and I began to feel a bit better.

The hamburger was an effort, though. I'd ordered the smallest size, but it was still hard, when I was with Larry, to feel relaxed enough to eat. He finished mine off for me, and my fries. But I managed the whole milkshake. I'd probably get through the evening without fainting. Although when it came to that goodnight kiss . . . I thought it would be nice to gaze into Larry's eyes, for a minute, but he was staring out of the window again. I had to think of something to say.

"Lorette says we shouldn't eat hamburgers," I said, suddenly remembering what she'd told me a couple of weeks ago.

"What's up? Scared of getting too fat?" Larry grinned. I didn't like the sound of that. *Too* fat. It sounded as if he thought I was quite fat already. "Don't worry," he squeezed my hand again. "I like girls to be a bit cuddly, something to grab hold of. You're just about perfect."

All at once I felt like a million dollars. My head spun, my heart went into second gear and a ridiculous grin spread right across my face. It was such a fantastic feeling when he said things like that to me. Everything else went out of my mind and all I could think was, *I'm just about perfect. Larry Payne thinks I'm just about perfect. Me! Perfect! so there.*

"What were you saying?" asked Larry.

"What *was* I saying?" (I panicked.)

"About hamburgers." (I was still mystified.)

"What about hamburgers?"

"Your friend Lorraine."

"Lorette! Oh yeah! Well, she says we shouldn't eat hamburgers because of the rainforests."

"You what?" Larry looked puzzled. I tried hard to remember the facts.

"Well apparently they cut down the rainforests."

"Yeah, yeah, I know all about that," Larry said, impatiently, as if I was being a bore. It was confusing. One minute I was just about perfect, the next I was boring. Life was getting really complicated these days.

"Well, you see, it's ... I think it's ... " My mind went blank. How did the blasted rainforests relate to the hamburgers?

"Get on with it. You'll have me falling asleep."

I tried hard to hear Lorette's voice and the words she'd used.

"Oh, yes. They cut down the rainforests to make room to graze cattle. But the grass is so poor, the only sort of cows who can survive there end up as hamburgers. So these hamburger people are partly responsible for the cutting down of the rainforests."

"Blimey. You'll have me howling in a minute. Look, we've got to eat, haven't we?"

"Yes, but, well, maybe not hamburgers."

"But you've just had one yourself."

"I know." I was getting very uncomfortable. "But maybe I shouldn't have." Larry yawned and put his jacket on. "It's just something Lorette said," I went on, but then that sounded a bit too apologetic. "It made me think, though."

Larry got up.

"That Lorette, she's a bad influence on you," he said as we went out. I stopped, open-mouthed, in the High Street. Lorette, a bad influence on me! Lorette, with her high ideals, and her careful diets and her athletics training, and her good grades in school and her — well — really strong morality. Lorette, a bad influence?

"What?" I just gawped. "*Lorette?*"

"Yeah," said Larry, kicking a Coke can into the road. "She's one of these extremists, isn't she? Wants power to the people and all that crap. Mob rule, that's what she's after. You want to watch your step. You'd be better off not mixed up with people like that."

I was stunned. I simply couldn't believe it. I

walked along for the next hundred yards in silence. How could Lorette possibly be a bad influence on me? Why, even my mum had said once that the problem was that *I* was likely to be a bad influence on *her*.

"Don't you like Lorette, then?" I asked, taking his hand as we crossed the road.

"Oh, I like her fine," he said casually, admiring a leather jacket in a shop window as we passed. "Wait a minute. I want to see how much that is." I waited whilst he looked at the price of everything.

"Think it'd suit me?" he asked.

"Oh yes!" My foolish smile was back. "But then, I think you'd look great in anything."

Larry smiled to himself, and put his arm round me as we moved off. I sort of snuggled up as close to him as I could — quite hard to do really, if you're walking along. It felt nice, walking so close. And he had said he liked Lorette. But I couldn't leave it alone. I just wanted to confirm it, somehow.

"You do like Lorette then, Larry? Really?"

"Oh sure," said Larry casually, watching a girl motorcyclist going past in a skin-tight red leather bike suit. "Except that they're not really like us, are they?"

"What do you mean, they?"

"You know. Darkies."

I couldn't speak again till we got to the Empire.

The evening should've been great. There was a really funny supporting group called *Excuse Me*, and then *Carnivorous*. They really know how to sing, those guys. They're my favourites. But all the time I should've been listening to the music, I was in turmoil. My feet were tapping along to the rhythm, but my mind was stuck, it couldn't let go. It couldn't stop thinking about what Larry had said. What he'd called Lorette.

All the way home I felt really low. Larry was chatting on about the leather jacket he was going to get for his birthday, and whether the one we'd seen in the High Street would be best. Or should he go to a little shop his brother knew, down near Aldgate? I tried to take an interest, but I couldn't. I felt kind of sick and uneasy, as if I'd eaten something that had disagreed with me. Larry didn't seem to notice how preoccupied I was.

When we stopped by my door, I suddenly knew I was going to say something. I couldn't stop myself.

"I hated what you said about Lorette," I burst out. "What you called her."

Larry looked astonished.

"Hey! Hold on, kid. Keep your hair on. It was only a joke."

"Was it?"

" 'Course it was, dumbo. I know she's your best mate and she's a great athlete. I was just kidding you along. OK?"

"OK." I was still very doubtful, but then Larry put it all out of my mind by more or less jumping on me.

His tongue was in my mouth, my ears, round my neck. He seemed to have as many tongues as a whole shopful of trainers. It all took me a bit by surprise. I wished he'd slow down and take it easy. Then I could have got interested. I felt sort of left behind. I wanted to go back to the beginning and start again. And I'd have liked to look into his eyes first, for a while, and for him to say a few things about how perfect I was. Then maybe start the kissing, nice and slow at first.

But if I was left at the starting post, Larry was over the horizon. His breath blasted into my ear.

"You're such a turn-on," he panted, "such a turn-on, Jane!"

He was getting out of control. I had to slap him down, like a dog jumping up after the biscuits.

"I gotta go, Larry. Or I'll be in trouble. It's late. Thanks for a great evening. See yah."

I tore myself away and went up the steps two at a time, afraid that he might follow.

By the time Mum got in, I was in bed. There was a livid pink love-bite on my neck and I didn't want Mum to see it. I was going to have to wear a scarf for the next few days. It made me angry.

I heard Mum come in, and I switched out my light and made sure I was lying on the love-bite side. Mum tapped at the door.

"Jane, love! Are you still awake?"

"Yes, Mum. Did you have a nice time?"

She crept in, and sat on my bed in the dark.

"It was really nice, Jane. I laughed so much my ribs ache. And we saw this fascinating film. Made in India."

I squeezed Mum's hand.

"Great, Mum. I'm so glad."

Mum bent down and kissed me on the cheek; a gentle little dry warm kiss. Her nice Mum-smell nestled over my head, together with a whiff of the lovely spicy perfume I gave her for Christmas from Sudeshna's shop.

"Goodnight, Jane, love."

"Goodnight, Mum."

At the door she paused.

"I'm off my rocker. I forgot to ask. How was your date?"

"Terrific," I said, and closed my eyes tight. But I didn't sleep. Not for hours and hours and hours.

10

That Sunday I went into the park. It was funny kind of weather. One moment the sun was lighting up the whole world, making you feel that everything would turn out all right, and then suddenly these grey clouds would go scudding across and the cold wind would toss the leaves of the trees about. I wore my black zip-up top that goes right up to my chin, to hide the love-bite. I hoped it would fade soon. I'd put lots of moisturiser on it but it was still angry and purply-red.

Ginger Mike appeared, on roller-skates again. He swooped past me ever so close and made a funny kind of cutting movement with his hand across the top of my head, as if he was mowing my hair like grass.

"Hey, Mike!" I said. "Where *is* everybody?"

Mike swerved round and came back to where I was.

"Over there." He pointed to a clump of trees. "We're training Lorette. The trouble is, she can beat me even when I've got these skates on."

"Well, you're completely spastic," I said, giving him a push that sent him staggering off onto the grass, arms cartwheeling madly to keep his balance.

"Hey! You're getting strong!" he yelled. "Are you an alien or something?"

"It's just my training," I grinned, flexing my biceps at him.

I'd lost so much weight recently, you could actually tell where my muscles were. It was great. My jeans were now totally baggy. I mean, they'd always been supposed to be baggy, but what with my hips and legs being so baggy until recently, the jeans had been too tight in all the wrong places. In fact — don't tell anybody — but they used to give me a sore bum. Isn't that heroic? I've suffered for fashion, believe me.

Ginger Mike held on to my shoulders and I sort of pulled him along like a lorry towing a car that's broken down. It was odd, how different I felt when Ginger Mike touched me, from the way Larry Payne made me feel. Ginger Mike was just like an old teddy bear. It was the same kind of touching as a child sitting on your knee. I suppose that's how you feel if you've got a brother or a dad to cuddle. My body wasn't in the slightest bit interested in Mike. It felt sort of asleep.

Whereas Larry — of course, holding his hand was a terrific feeling. And when he kissed me, well, if only he'd slow down a bit and take a bit more time over it, it'd be magic. I expect I wasn't used to this kissing business yet. I was sure I'd get used to it, in time. As long as I got lots and lots of practice. I just hoped and prayed that Larry wouldn't go off me and take somebody else out instead. I just couldn't stand that. I think I'd die.

"There they are," said Ginger Mike as we came up to the trees. A little group of people was sitting on the grass with their backs to us. Wayne was there, Sudeshna was there, and — but then my eyes played a funny trick on me. For a moment it looked just as if Andy Fowler was sitting with his back to me — *with his arm round Lorette*! I blinked once. I blinked twice. I stood stock still. And do you know what? *It was true*!

Yes, Andy Fowler *was* sitting with his arm round Lorette. Once I realised it was true, once I'd sort of taken it in, something really weird happened. My mouth went suddenly completely dry, as if my spit had all run away down a plughole somewhere. And my eyes — well, they *sizzled*. I know it sounds odd — but for a minute I thought I was going to faint. There was a sort of roaring in my ears, and a funny kind of sick feeling went rushing down from my ears to ny ankles. I grabbed the tree to steady myself.

"Hey! Little hedgehog!" called Wayne. Everybody looked round.

"Hi, Jane!" beamed Lorette. She looked really pleased to see me. Andy Fowler looked round too, and as he did, the arm that had been round Lorette went off to scratch his head, and didn't go back. From above, what with me standing up, I could see that his hair looked just like brown fur. I wondered what it would feel like to run your hand across it. Had Lorette tried that yet? I tried to grin, but I was tongue-tied and couldn't speak.

"Cheer up!" said Andy. "It may never happen!"

"It already has!" I said, sitting down beside them.

"What has?" asked Lorette.

"Nothing. Only kidding."

"What's wrong with you?" Andy Fowler studied

my face. I wished he wouldn't. "You look different. Had a face lift?"

"She's lost a lot of weight," said Lorette. "Ain't you, Jane?"

"I know the best way to lose weight," said Ginger Mike. "Cut your head off."

Sudeshna gave a little scream.

"You been on a diet, then?" asked Andy Fowler. "Haven't seen you in the shop recently."

"No," I said. "I didn't go on a diet. It just sort of fell off."

"It fell off the back of a lorry," said Ginger Mike. "Or, in Jane's case, it fell off the back of a bus." I thumped him. It made me feel better. Ginger Mike should be available for thumping on the National Health Service.

"Well, I think it's a big mistake," said Andy Fowler.

"I don't!" said Wayne, who had been leaning on his elbow, watching us. "She looks great. Take no notice, sister. He's just takin' the piss."

I tried to smile gratefully at Wayne, but my mouth wouldn't behave properly.

"It wouldn't be so bad if she cheered up," said Andy Fowler. "You look like a wet weekend, what's up?" It was hard to say. Something was up — definitely. But I hardly dared look closely enough at it to see what it was. For a horrible minute I thought I was going to cry. My mouth kind of quivered. But I whipped out my hankie and blew my nose instead.

"Blimey! Not so loud!" said Andy Fowler. "It's like the bleedin' Trumpet Voluntary."

"There's nothing wrong with Jane, anyway," said Lorette. "She's going out with Larry Payne, so!" She said it sort of *at* Andy.

"I know. I know." Andy gave her a private and mischievous grin. "Lucky girl."

"Lucky Larry!" said Wayne, and his big brown eyes sent me such a doggy look, I was tempted for a moment to throw him a stick.

"*Larry Payne and Jane Watts,*" said Ginger Mike in a film soundtrack kind of voice. "*They called them the Perfect Couple. By day they were just Larry and Jane, a regular guy and his gal. But by night they were . . . the Vampires!*"

He gave a loud bloodcurdling scream and slumped over onto the grass.

"Watch out," said Lorette. "You just missed that dog shit."

I'd never seen Ginger Mike sit up so fast. He stared at the grass. It was perfectly clean. The others laughed.

"Only kidding," said Lorette.

"*It looked like ordinary dog shit . . .* " said Mike, still in his Hollywood voice. "*But little did the world suspect that this was . . . the Dog Shit from Outer Space!*"

Lorette got up and danced about a bit.

"I'm ready to do a bit more," she said.

Andy got to his feet too. We all scrambled up.

"I've got to go, Lorette. Sorry," said Sudeshna. "My mum will be mad."

"I'll see you home for a Mars bar," said Ginger Mike.

"*Mars bars — the chocolate treat from Another Planet!*"

"All right," Sudeshna smiled. "You can see me home, Mike."

"It's no good, Ginger Mike," I said. "She's going to marry this guy in India. What's his name, Sudeshna? It's all fixed up."

Sudeshna blushed and looked angry.

"Shut up, Jane. Good luck, Lorette. See you tomorrow."

Then she went. Ginger Mike followed, hoping for his bar from the planet Mars.

I felt really bad about mentioning Sudeshna's arranged marriage. Perhaps none of the others knew about it. She'd looked very embarrassed, as if I'd betrayed her or let a big secret out. I felt miserable and guilty. And the trouble was, I knew I'd done it for bad reasons. To have the limelight off me and onto somebody else. To make someone else embarrassed instead of me. Fancy choosing gentle little Sudeshna! I felt as though I'd been a total bitch.

"Come on." Andy Fowler was suddenly right in front of me. "Snap out of it. I'm going to run with her. Here's the stop watch."

As he handed it to me, his fingers brushed the palm of my hand, and suddenly the park turned a complete somersault, so the grass went flashing over our heads and the sky beneath our feet. The funny thing was, nobody else seemed to notice. Then everything settled down and was ordinary again. I looked at the stop watch and panicked.

"I don't know how to work these things!"

"I'll help you. Give it here." Wayne took it from me, and started it off as Lorette set off down the path like a bullet, with Andy at her side. Wayne and I watched them disappear round the far side of the lake.

"Wayne," I began, but I didn't know how to put it. "Is Andy — is Lorette . . . are Andy and Lorette going out together?"

"Looks that way," said Wayne. "Great, isn't it?" I couldn't speak.

It was great, of course. Lorette deserved to have somebody special to take care of her. And Andy was special — there was no denying it. But my mouth had started to wobble again. I bit my lip.

"Hey, little hedgehog!" Wayne put his arm around me in a kind, brotherly way. "What's wrong? That Larry Payne not treatin' you right? Remember what I said. I'm your bodyguard. If that guy puts a foot wrong — if he harms a hair on your head — he's a dead man." He was half-joking. I managed to shake my head and crank up something like a smile.

"No, no, Wayne — don't worry. It's great. He's terrific. I'm really happy."

Wayne looked at me very soberly for a second.

"You can't fool me, Jane Watts," he said. "You got trouble in your eyes, sister. What is it?"

Luckily I was saved by Lorette who came storming into view around the bandstand. So Wayne had to sort the stop watch out.

"Fantastic!" he yelled, as she flew past. "Best yet!" Then Andy came up, panting, so we couldn't do dangerous talk any more. But I could see clearly that I wasn't going to be able to hide the truth from Wayne much longer. Whatever the truth was. I was doing a pretty good job, at the moment, of hiding it from myself.

Next time I saw Wayne was Monday morning. He usually goes to school by bike, but today he was waiting at the bus stop.

"Hi!" I said. "Where's Lorette?"

"Man, she's really sick," Wayne shook his head. "It's this headache, see? She's got it so bad she can't bear the daylight. She's in bed with the curtains drawn an' an icepack on her head."

"Oh no! And it's the trials on Saturday! I hope she'll be better by then."

"Sure to be," said Wayne, but he didn't look completely certain. "I mean, you ever hear of a headache lasting six days?"

"I expect it's the tension," I said, trying to imagine what it must be like to be Lorette, with such an important event coming up. "She's such a perfectionist."

"Yeah." Wayne grinned, yawned and stretched. "Too bad it doesn't run in the family. I'm an imperfectionist. That's why I like you so much."

I punched him on the belly button, but he saw it coming and flexed all his muscles.

"Not bad, sister," he grinned, pulling my hair very gently. "How's your self-defence coming along?"

"OK."

I was beginning to wonder when I was going to

need it, what with old Mrs Weldon being attacked, and then Sudeshna's dad. Oh hell. I remembered how upset Sudeshna had been when I mentioned her arranged marriage. I'd really have to make it up with her today.

"OK, what's cookin'?" asked Wayne. "You got one huge frown on your pretty little face, Jane."

The bus came and we got on.

"I was horrible to Sudeshna yesterday. I teased her about — you know, that guy she's going to marry."

"What guy?"

"Somebody in India. She's going to have an arranged marriage. Didn't you know about that?"

"I thought you were just kidding around."

"No. She's got his photo in her wallet and everything. She showed me."

"I couldn't handle that," said Wayne. "Havin' my wife chosen for me. I know who they'd choose, an' all. Grace Joseph." And he laughed softly to himself.

"Who's Grace Joseph?"

"Doesn't matter. My mum and dad think she's a real star. But I don't go for her at all. She's not my idea of a tutti frutti."

"Who *is* your idea of a tutti frutti?"

Wayne winked at me.

"A little fat girl with spiky hair. Who's crazy about somebody else."

I pretended to scratch his hand, like an angry cat.

"I thought you said I wasn't fat? Yesterday when Andy — "

112

"Look, Jane, I like you the way you are, and I liked you the way you were. I don't give a shit whether you're size ten or size fourteen. I like you. OK?"

Wayne began to look a bit too serious. I had to change the subject, and fast.

"What's all this with Lorette and Andy Fowler, then?"

"What's it to you, little hedgehog?"

"It's nothing to me. I'm just interested, that's all."

I blushed, though. My whole face went hot and it stayed hot for ages. Wayne looked at me very carefully and shook his head.

"I thought you were crazy for Larry."

"I am! For heaven's sake! Well, maybe not crazy, exactly, I mean . . . "

I looked out of the window. I didn't really know what I did mean, to tell you the truth. I realised that ever since I'd seen Andy with his arm round Lorette, I hadn't thought much about Larry Payne at all. I suppose it was a bit of a shock. I mean, Lorette's my best mate, and she's never had any time for boys before. It's important when your best friend gets a boyfriend for the first time. I suppose that's why I was so amazed. And I certainly didn't expect it to be Andy Fowler. But of course, why not?

Lorette really deserves a break. She can be kind of hard on herself. Andy was the perfect guy for her, really — he was such a comedian. He'd loosen her up and help her to relax. He'd be kind and supportive and he was strong and independent, too.

And playful. In fact, I couldn't think of anyone better for Lorette, and I was really pleased for her. So why did my insides feel as if they were tied in a knot?

"Will you practise my self-defence with me at lunchtime?" I asked Wayne. I knew I'd feel better if I could wrestle a bit with somebody.

"Sure." Wayne was still staring at me. I wished he wouldn't. I really liked him — *but*. "Listen, Jane, what's makin' you so unhappy? This Larry guy not treating you right? Shall I fill him in for you?"

"No, really, Wayne — he's great. Everything's fine. I'm just a bit low at the moment, that's all."

Wayne sighed and turned away. He wasn't satisfied, I could tell. I wasn't all that satisfied myself.

At school Ginger Mike came up to me in the yard.

"Come behind the boiler house with me," he ordered.

"Oh Mike!" I did a pretend giggle. "This is so sudden."

There were a few minutes to go before the bell, so I went behind the boiler house. You never know, with Ginger Mike. One day he might really find an alien, and then if you'd refused to go and see, you'd miss it. But it wasn't aliens that Ginger Mike had on the brain today.

Once he'd made sure nobody was around, he got an envelope out of his pocket, and shook a little white powder into the palm of his hand.

"See that?" he whispered reverently. "Ace stuff.

Top quality coke. Fresh off the plane from San Francisco."

"You're a berk, Mike."

"No. Really, try some. Snort it."

I bent forward, and gave it a gentle little sniff. Don't get me wrong. I'd never have dreamed of doing that if it had really been coke. I just wanted to see what it was, icing sugar or what. It had a lemony smell and it tickled my nose. Then I dipped my little finger in and tasted a bit. It was one of those powders you take when you've got a cold — you know, aspirin and lemon and stuff.

"It's a Beecham's Powder, Mike. You've been at your mum's bathroom cabinet again."

"Hey! Don't say that! This is ace dope. Don't say they cut it with something. This guy — my dealer — he *promised* me . . ."

Ginger Mike bent down and sniffed hard. You're supposed to use a tube of paper — at least that's what they did in the Woody Allen film — but Mike had forgotten that. He just took a deep sniff, and then did such a big sneeze, it nearly knocked the boiler house over.

"Yeah! You're right. They've cut it with something. Just wait till I see that guy — *Aaaa choo!*"

I shook my head — Ginger Mike's unbelievable, sometimes. I think it's the jargon he really goes for, not the drugs at all. He spends all his time glued to the video and he speaks fluent film-talk of all sorts.

"*Aaaa choo!* Have you got a tissue, Jane?"

I gave him one. But he was still sneezing, and his eyes were streaming ten minutes later when

Obergruppenführer Fischer took the register. It's really dangerous stuff, that cold and 'flu powder.

At break I cornered Sudeshna by the science block. I had to apologise.

"Sudeshna!" I grabbed her sleeve. "I'm really sorry about what I said yesterday. I didn't think. Honestly. It must've been so embarrassing for you. How can I make it up to you?" Sudeshna smiled and squeezed my arm.

"Hi! Oh, it's OK, Jane. I didn't mind, really. I was just a bit surprised, that's all."

"Well of course! It was stupid of me. Let's sit down on this wall. Look! I've got some special curry-flavoured crisps for you."

We sat down on the wall and I opened the packet. Sudeshna was so sweet and forgiving. Like that Indian bloke — Gandhi. Did you see the film? It was on TV. He was forgiving and non-violent all his life, and then in the end someone shot him.

I find it really hard to be non-violent. If somebody gets under my skin, or makes me mad, I go all sort of hot and out of control. But here was Sudeshna being all quiet and serene and understanding. I really admired her. But I couldn't be like that myself, not in a million years.

"How are you getting on with Larry, Jane?" asked Sudeshna. I scrunched up the crisp packet and tossed it towards the bin. It missed.

"Oh, great. Fantastic."

"What's he like?"

I thought for a minute.

"Well, he's really . . . " my voice tailed off. I thought of the times I'd been with Larry, and all

116

the things he'd said. And somehow it didn't seem to add up.

"He's quite hard to get to know. In a way. He's, you know, mysterious."

That made me feel better. It sounded OK. It sounded exciting.

" . . . And he's very, well, ambitious. I mean, not too ambitious. But he's got plans for the future." Sudeshna nodded and waited for more. What could I tell her? Some of the things Larry had said, I'd rather forget. But strangely enough, those were the ones that I couldn't get out of my mind.

The way he'd talked about Sudeshna's dad, for instance. But then, he'd said he'd only been kidding. And then, all that about Lorette being a bad influence on me.

"Is he mad about you, Jane?" Sudeshna giggled shyly. She was terrifically interested in it all, of course. Even more interested because it was something she'd never be able to experience, herself. Mind you, I sort of envied her her photo in the wallet, the idea that her parents were going to fix her up with that guy with the smouldering eyes. It certainly simplified things. Being free to go out with whoever you like was terribly confusing at times.

"Is he mad about me? I shouldn't think so." I laughed — a bit nervously. "What I can't understand is what he saw in me in the first place."

"Oh yeah?" said a voice behind us. "Who's this you're talking about?"

We turned round. It was Larry Payne. I went red. So did Sudeshna. Neither of us could say a word for a minute. Then I recovered.

"Hey, Larry!" I began. "Guess what! Lorette's ill, and it's only five days till the trials. Isn't it awful? We're all really worried."

"She'll be better in time," he said. "You bet. I don't suppose she'd miss it if she was in intensive care."

"Are you coming?" I asked suddenly. It would be great if Larry could come. Maybe he could get to know the gang properly. And I'd feel better about seeing Lorette and Andy together if I had Larry by my side.

"Saturday afternoon?" He thought for a minute. "No. Sorry. There's something I've got to do. But if you fancy coming out in the evening, I'll be at the bus stop at eight."

"Oh yes. Right. Great." I grinned. He sort of rubbed my shoulder and strolled off. Seeing him reminded me of the love-bite. I'd put seven layers of make-up on it that morning and it was just about invisible — although at least three of the seven layers had come off on my collar. I hoped Sudeshna wouldn't notice.

"I'm really scared of him," she said when he'd gone. "I don't know why."

"Don't be silly, Sudeshna," I scolded her. All the same, I sort of knew what she meant.

At lunchtime I attacked Wayne. Or rather, he attacked me, and I defended myself. All the same, it was pretty obvious that somebody big and strong could probably overpower me. I'm a bit awkward physically, and uncoordinated, and I wasn't finding the self-defence classes all that easy, to tell you the truth.

"Listen, babe," said Wayne after I'd beaten him off once and failed twice. "What you gotta do, see — if a guy attacks you, kick him in the goolies. Or use your knee. It's simple but effective."

"Really?" I grinned. "Shall we have a practice, then?"

"No thanks!" Wayne skipped away. "I don't love you that much, sister."

The bell went for the end of lunch.

"Saved by the bell," grinned Wayne. "So long. You're doing well. But if it ever comes to it, let him have it where it hurts. Don't hesitate. Promise me."

"OK. I promise."

And I drifted off to English, wondering if Lorette would be better in time for the trials. I wasn't really thinking about Wayne's advice at all. I just had to hope that if I ever got in trouble my instincts would come to the rescue. And I was going to need my instincts much sooner than I thought.

12

Well, the great day dawned. The minute I woke up, I felt excited. Lorette's big day! I put on my tracksuit sort of in sympathy. I never used to dare to wear it in the old days when my bum was so huge it used to blot out the sun. Now it had shrunk down a lot and the tracksuit looked all right. I don't suppose anyone would ever mistake me for an athlete, though.

Before breakfast I rang Lorette and asked how she was feeling.

"Fine," she said. "A bit tense, maybe. But OK."

We fixed up to meet — the whole gang was coming along to the stadium — and I told her to have lots of scrambled eggs for breakfast to build her up, and rang off.

Mum was singing in the kitchen. The sun came streaming through the window and made rainbows in the steam from the kettle. It was an old Bob Dylan number. Mum was a Bob Dylan addict when she was young. And she'd started playing all his old LPs again recently. Most of them were scratched, but she didn't care. I like the words. He's a real poet, that Dylan.

"You going out with Andy Fowler's dad again tonight, Mum?"

"Yes, we thought we'd go down the West End

and see that film that's just opened. You know, with Dustin Hoffman."

"Hey! Fantastic! Wish I could come."

"Well, why don't you? We could get Andy along too. Have a double date across the generations. That'd be fun!" Mum laughed to herself, juggling hot toast from the grill. I had to knock this idea on the head, right away.

"Don't be silly, Mum! Andy's going out with Lorette." Mum paused, halfway to the fridge.

"Is he really? Good for him. You surprise me, though. His dad was telling me only last week that he reckoned Andy's got a soft spot for you."

Another appalling blush broke out. I was even blushing on top of my head, under the hair. Quick as a flash I bent down to re-tie my trainers. It's a good excuse, you see, for having a red face.

"No, Mum, it's Lorette he goes for," I said to the floor. "And anyway, I'm still going out with Larry, don't forget."

"Ah well," said Mum with a sigh, "it takes all sorts, I suppose." I wonder what she meant by that?

I was determined not to think about Andy having a soft spot for me. I didn't think about it all the way down Essex Road, on the bus. Then I got on the Underground and I didn't think about it all the way to the stadium. *Hell's bells*, I thought as I pushed my way in through the gates, *I've got to stop not thinking about it soon or I'll be face to face with him. Or rather, them.*

Luckily I met Ginger Mike, who distracted me, and told me where everyone was.

"Hey! Wow! It's like the Olympics!" he said.

"And there's a breathless hush as the girls get down on their blocks . . . here's the British girl, Lorette Winstone, she looks nervous, but I'm willing to bet, ladies and gentlemen, that today's the day that A Star will be Born."

I managed to shut him up, and he led me to where our little gang was. We'd got some places right down by the track. It couldn't have been in a better position. Lorette was jogging up and down in her tracksuit. I sat down next to Sudeshna and Wayne. Andy was leaning on the barrier and trying to say something to Lorette. Then she saw me and came over.

"Hi, Jane," she said.

"Hi, Lorette. How do you feel?"

"OK. But I got a bit of a headache. I wish I had an aspirin or somethin'. You got one?" She massaged her brows. "It's the tension."

"I know. Oh dear, I haven't. But — wait! Mike! You've got some aspirins, haven't you?"

"To what do you allude, dear madam?"

"C'mon. Stop mucking about. Lorette's got a headache. Give her one of your pills or powders or whatever."

"What, in broad daylight? In public? My dear girl, I do not wish to be arrested before the multitude."

"Shut up and get your headache pills out."

"Go on, Mike — please!" Lorette can be very persuasive when she fixes you with her beady eye.

Mike reached inside his pocket, and brought out an envelope. Inside were some pills. He gave her two. Lorette looked at them suspiciously.

122

"You sure they're headache pills?"

"Of course they are, Lorette. He nicks them from his mum's bathroom cabinet. Don't you, Mike?"

"I cannot reveal my sources."

He didn't need to. We all knew where Mike got his so-called "drugs" from. So Lorette took the pills, and washed them down with a carton of orange juice provided by Andy.

"You think of everything," said Lorette to him, sort of privately, and they just looked at each other for a minute as if they were all alone in the world and none of the rest of us was there.

"Where's lover-boy?" said Wayne in my ear.

"He couldn't come. He had something he had to do."

"Sure, sure."

Wayne was sitting with his hands in his pockets, looking very tense. Andy was talking to Lorette in her ear as if he was her coach. He hadn't even said hello to me yet. But why should he?

"Want a Mars bar, Jane?" asked Sudeshna. I suddenly felt empty inside.

"Yes, Sudeshna," I said. "Yes, I blasted well would. Thanks ever so."

The Mars bar made my teeth jump and I felt a bit sick afterwards, but what the hell.

Lorette had gone off and was getting some last-minute coaching from Mrs Andrews.

"Mrs Andrews is really fit, for someone middle-aged," I said.

"Middle-aged?" laughed Wayne. "She's only about thirty-five."

"Well, what *is* middle-aged, then?"

123

"My mum's middle-aged," said Ginger Mike. "I was a late baby. Several other geniuses have been, too."

"Is she fit?" asked Wayne. "Can she run up and down like Mrs Andrews, and kick her legs in the air?"

"You must be joking," said Mike. "She tried to redecorate the bathroom last week. It's the smallest room you've ever seen. But guess what — she ends up with tennis elbow."

"How can you get tennis elbow from decorating?" I asked.

"By waving a paintbrush about, dummy." I shrugged. It seemed a bit unlikely to me.

At last Lorette's event came round. In a way it's the hardest event of the lot — the 400 metres. You need all the stamina for the long distance and you have to be able to go like the clappers just like in the sprints. But Lorette could do it. She was great. Andy was sitting right on the edge of his seat, holding onto the barrier so hard that his knuckles had gone all white. Wayne and Sudeshna and I were all sort of clutching at each other, frozen in terror. And even Ginger Mike was sitting still. He'd switched his Walkman off, too. Quite a tribute to Lorette.

They got down on their blocks. An instant hush filled the stadium. My heart was in my mouth. It didn't taste too good, either. *On your marks* . . . All our hearts stopped beating in unison. Mine just lay right there on my tongue. *Get set* . . . Even the sky went still. The clouds froze. BANG!

They were off. We all jumped up and screamed

and screamed. Lorette had flashed off round the bend like a greyhound. We could see her cruising along the straight stretch opposite. But a big girl with blonde curls was out in the lead.

"C'mon, Lorette! You've got her on the run!"

"C'mon, *Lorette*! Go, go, go!"

She was gaining on her. Coming round the far bend we could see it clearly. Lorette's brown thighs were flashing in the sunlight, pounding and pounding like mad. Her eyes were wild — you could see the whites all round. I screamed one final scream, as if by one supreme effort I could give her every ounce of my strength.

"Lorette!" I shrieked, so hard I felt my tonsils tear.

Lorette's face went all kind of twisted and desperate, and with one last crazy surge of strength she half-fell, half-flew through the air and burst through the tape a fraction of an inch ahead.

"She did it! She did it! She won!"

Wayne threw me in the air. Sudeshna burst into tears. Ginger Mike beat his chest and howled like Tarzan. And Andy vaulted right over the barrier and ran across to Lorette and gave her the biggest hug anyone's ever had — lifted her right off her feet and whirled her round and round. Even Mrs Andrews hugged her. My ears were bursting with glorious noise.

She'd done it, she'd done it, my best buddy had done it — she'd won, she'd made it, she was a star, it was the Big Time from here on in.

The loudspeakers were booming and the cheers and shouts were mingling with bells, horns, Coke cans being knocked together. It was definitely the race of the afternoon. Hell, it was the race of the *century*. Lorette was in the British Under 18 team now, that was a certainty. I couldn't believe it. She'd be travelling — maybe all over the world. I was so glad. She really deserved it, for all her hard work.

She deserved Andy too. I could see them walking along together, Lorette dazed and sort of stunned, Andy absolutely thrilled to bits. From time to time they gave each other a look, but they didn't say anything. They didn't need to. Lucky Lorette. She'd hit the jackpot, all right, in every possible way. And it couldn't have happened to a nicer person.

For a few days we were all walking on air. Then, all of a sudden, one evening, it happened. I was feeling pretty good, because Larry had just rung to fix up a date for later — around 8.30. Then the phone rang again. It was Ginger Mike. "Listen!" he hissed. "We've got to go to Lorette's. She had a dope test after her race and they've just got the result back. It's positive!"

13

We all went round to Lorette's house, of course. Lorette and Wayne live in Wilkinson Street and as we walked up the garden path we could already hear Lorette's mum wailing.

"What are we going to do? Oh, Henry! What am I going to say to Pastor King?"

We crowded inside. Lorette's mum was crying, and alternately dabbing her eyes, and fanning herself with an enormous hankie with butterflies embroidered on it.

"Never mind about Pastor King!" yelled Lorette's dad. "Get yourself under control, Gloria! C'mon now. Lorette needs our help and we gotta work out what we can do."

"We can't do anything, though! What can we do? Who's goin' to take notice of us? Who ever *has*?"

Mrs Winstone threw up her hands in an I-give-up sort of way, and another huge tear rolled down her nice round cheek. I felt really sorry for her.

Lorette was sitting at the table, dead silent, just sort of staring at the salt cellar. She'd got it in her hand and she was turning, turning, turning it round and round. I'd never seen her look so — well — zombie like. When we came in she sort of looked up at us, but her eyes went through us. It was really odd. Especially when I remembered what she'd looked like after winning the race — sort of bounding along, her face all lit up, with Andy at her side.

"What can we do, Mr Winstone?" asked Andy. But Lorette didn't seem to listen as he spoke.

"We gotta take this to court! We've gotta do it, Gloria! I won't rest, I tell you, till this whole thing's cleared up. Nobody gets away with this! Nobody gets away with framing my girl!"

Mr Winstone's eyes flashed, and he strode up and down the room liked a caged tiger. We tried to keep out of his way. He had such a ferocious look in his eye, I was sure he could've eaten any of us up on the spot, if we'd said the wrong thing.

"I'll go to the highest court! I'll go to the House of Lords! I'll go to the European Court of Justice!" he raged. Mrs Winstone just shrugged and sighed.

"Oh Henry, don't be such a child! How you going to pay the legal costs? Going to law is not for people like us, darlin'. You're living in a fool's paradise. Where we goin' to find that sort of money?"

"Don't talk to me about money!" yelled Lorette's dad, and he flung his arms in the air so hard, he knocked the lampshade and it swung to and fro like a jellyfish under water on the waves.

"I'm not interested in the money! Forget the money, Gloria, we got our reputation in the mud now here. Thirty-five years since I came to this country and never any trouble till now. And now this!"

"Sit down, sit down, you goin' to break the house up, Henry!" moaned Lorette's mum as he threw his arms about again and knocked a candlestick flying. I could see where Lorette got her fiery streak, her way of getting worked up about things, her fighting spirit. But she wasn't fighting now. She sat sort of slumped in her chair whilst her mum and dad argued, and all the shine had gone out of her.

Since we'd all come in, Mr and Mrs Winstone hadn't let up. In fact they hadn't even stopped for a second to say hello. I thought perhaps we were in the way and should go.

"Maybe we'd better push off!" I whispered to Wayne. Mrs Winstone heard and caught hold of my arm.

"No, darlin', you stay. I'm sorry we're so upset here, we haven't said hello or anything."

"But aren't we in the way?"

"No, no, no! It's real good of you to come and be with us in our trouble, Jane. You're a good girl. You're all good children."

Mrs Winstone sniffed a bit and held my hand against her cheek. There was a moment's silence. Mr Winstone was growling to himself as he leafed through the phone book.

"How did it happen?" I asked timidly.

Everybody looked at Lorette. But she didn't speak. She just sort of tilted her head on one side and closed her eyes.

"They announced they were going to do a test, right after the race," said Andy. "Mrs Andrews was told to take Lorette down to the lab. We thought it was just routine. Then, today, they said Lorette's test had showed up positive. They took another

129

sample and told her she was disqualified. That was it."

"But what — " I hesitated. "What did they find?"

"Steroids," said Andy.

Lorette opened her eyes and rolled them up to heaven. Her mum burst out again.

"But *how*, Lorette — how they manage to *find* that stuff in you, darlin'?"

For a minute Lorette's eyes went wide and wild, and she sort of showed her teeth.

"How many times I got to tell you, Gloria?" yelled Lorette's dad. "That's not a question you gotta ask *our daughter*. She don't know, somebody else knows, sure, but not Lorette."

"They dope racehorses, sometimes, don't they?" I said, suddenly remembering a TV programme I'd seen.

"That's right," said Andy. "Somebody must've done this on purpose."

"But why?"

"Somebody's jealous," said Lorette's dad. "Somebody can't stand it that my daughter gets in the British team."

"A conspiracy!" said Ginger Mike.

"Doesn't have to be a conspiracy," said Wayne. "Just one crazy person."

"But how would he *do* it?" I asked. I still didn't see how anyone could have fixed Lorette like that. There was a short pause. Then —

"O God!" said Sudeshna softly. "Mike's pills!"

It was quite something for Sudeshna to say *O God*. But I think you'll agree that this time, she had a real good excuse.

"What pills?" snapped Lorette's dad, whirling round on Mike. Mike's mouth opened, but no words came out. I could see he was wondering which bit of him Lorette's dad would eat first.

"Lorette had a headache," I explained. "Mike gave her some headache pills."

"Are you damn sure they were headache pills, boy?" roared Lorette's dad. Mike went very pale and his freckles sort of trembled. He nodded.

" 'Cos if they weren't — if you've been playing stupid games, I tell you, I won't be held responsible for my actions!"

"*Henry!*" said Lorette's mum, grabbing her husband's sleeve. "Calm down. Leave the boy alone. He's not done anything. Come on, now."

"Mike always has aspirins," I explained quickly. "He gets them from his mum's medicine chest. So he can — " I nearly said, "so he can pretend to be a dope fiend," but then I realised that might not be the most tactful thing I could mention right now.

"He gives us pills when we have headaches," said Sudeshna quickly. "I had a toothache last week and he gave me one then."

"Was it just aspirin, boy? You sure?" said Lorette's dad.

"Y-yes," said Ginger Mike. "I'm sure. That's all my mum ever has. Aspirin."

Mr Winstone gave him a really tough look, and then went back to the telephone book; leafing through it, desperately looking for ideas, for someone who could help them.

After the business of Mike's pills I thought it was time we left. Sudeshna had to go home anyway — and Ginger Mike was keen to get as far away as possible from Lorette's dad's teeth. Andy stayed, though. Just as the rest of us were saying our goodbyes, Lorette suddenly looked up at him and if ever a look said, "Please stay!" that was it. So he stayed.

I felt a bit funny about that. If I didn't know how ridiculous it was, I'd say I felt a bit jealous. But which one of them I was jealous *of*, I couldn't for the life of me tell.

"Well!" said Ginger Mike, once we were out in the street, "that was close. I thought he was going to vaporise me."

Sudeshna giggled.

"You are sure about those pills, aren't you, Mike?" I asked. Mike kicked a stone along the pavement. It was quite an effort for him to admit that his precious drugs were really only headache pills.

"Well . . . yes. Although the week before, I had some really high quality . . . "

"Oh shut up, Mike!" I said. "That joke's not funny any more."

I don't often tell Ginger Mike to shut up. So he did.

"Poor Lorette!" said Sudeshna. "Imagine how she felt."

"She didn't say a word, all the time we were there."

"I know. I think Andy will be very good to help her feel better. You know what I mean, Jane?"

I knew what she meant.

"Yeah."

132

"Isn't it funny about those two? Lorette — well, honestly I never thought she would have a boyfriend yet. She's always been so, well, serious, hasn't she? But this Andy — he really swept her off her feet."

I couldn't think of anything to say. Ginger Mike was tongue-tied with embarrassment, and I was tongue-tied with something else.

"Swept her off her feet, did he?" said Mike eventually. "What size was the brush?"

Nobody laughed.

"The way he looks at her sometimes, you know," Sudeshna sighed. "It's wonderful. As if she's some kind of angel. A black angel." She laughed. "The best sort!"

I tried to imagine Andy looking at someone as if they were any sort of angel. Somehow I got the feeling Sudeshna was getting a little carried away on a romantic wave. I wished she wouldn't.

"It makes me think, you know, Jane." Yes. Unfortunately. "It makes me wonder what it would be like to go out with an English boy. Really."

"Hey! Watch out! Remember what's his name. In your wallet," I whispered.

"Ladies, I must leave you," said Ginger Mike. We'd reached the end of his street, and he scooted off down it, really glad to be free of the boy-girl talk. One day Ginger Mike will fall in love — and they'll hear the crash fifty miles away.

"What would it be like, though?" said Sudeshna. "This business with Lorette and Andy — I can't stop thinking about it."

133

"So you fancy him, then?"

Sudeshna giggled.

"Oh no. He's much much too naughty for me. I prefer somebody serious. But he's just perfect for Lorette, isn't he, Jane? Just perfect."

I sighed.

"Yes," I agreed. "Just perfect."

We had reached Sudeshna's shop, and not before time. It was a relief to be on my own for the last two hundred yards home. A crescent moon was hanging in the sky, though it was still light.

It wasn't until I passed the bus stop by the chemist's that I remembered that I'd promised to meet Larry Payne here, an hour and a half ago. All that business with Lorette had driven it clean out of my mind. When I realised, I stopped dead in my tracks and went hot and cold with horror. I'd stood Larry up! What had he thought? What would he say? I broke into a run — I had to get home, and ring him up, right away. But as I hared up the steps, two at a time, my heart was heavy with dread. I had a horrible kind of feeling that this time I'd really blown it.

14

I let myself in, fumbling with the key, and ran to the phone. Mum was still out with Andy Fowler's dad, of course. So nobody would overhear me being crawling and apologetic. My heart was beating fast as I heard the phone ring in Larry's house. Maybe he wouldn't answer. Maybe he hadn't gone home after being stood up by me. It would be much more like him to stay out for the evening.

Wait though — someone picked the phone up and said hello. It was Larry!

"Larry — I'm so sorry about not turning up tonight. But something terrible happened."

"What?"

I told him all about how Lorette had had the drugs test, and how we'd all gone round to her house, and what a state her folks had been in . . . well, everything in fact.

" . . . and by the time I'd remembered our date, it was too late. I'm ever so sorry, Larry. Only all this business with Lorette just, well, put everything else out of my mind." I trembled, waiting for his reaction.

"Don't worry — it's OK."

He didn't mind.

"Oh Larry — that's ever so nice of you." He was kind! He was understanding! He was, he was, he was! "But I hate to think of you waiting around, Larry. I hope you didn't wait long."

"No! — it's OK. In fact, to tell you the truth I forgot about it myself."

"Oh did you? Oh, thank goodness. That makes me feel much better."

"Yeah. I was watching the video, see, and I fell asleep on the sofa, and when I woke up it was half past eight. I knew you'd have given up by then so I didn't bother to come out."

"Right. Well. That was lucky, wasn't it?"

"Yeah."

I felt relieved. So Larry hadn't been kept waiting. What a coincidence. It was really as if fate was on our side, quietly fixing things up for us.

"Er — well, see you on Monday then," I said. I didn't want to wait that long, but we'd only ever gone out on Saturday nights before. I'd had the impression that Sundays were sacred — a day devoted to the worship of the motorbike.

"Hey, wait! Not so fast. You don't escape that easily."

I loved it when he talked like that.

"What do you mean?"

"Well, why don't we get together tomorrow? You could come round here, if you like."

"What, to your place?"

"Sure. You've never been here, have you?"

"No, I haven't."

"Right. Come on over. Around noon. OK?"

He gave me the address. I didn't tell him that I knew it already, by heart. I'd looked it up in the phone book long before he'd ever spoken to me.

In fact, I'd even been curious enough to go and walk past it a few months back — just to see the house where the dishy Larry Payne lived. And now I was being invited there! At lunchtime, too. I was really looking forward to meeting his mum and dad. I went off into my bedroom to try and sort out something to wear.

After I'd tried on everything twice, I decided I hadn't got anything remotely suitable. I didn't want them to think I was the sort of girl who slopped around in jeans and T-shirts. On the other hand, I *was* the sort of girl who slopped around in jeans and T-shirts. I wished Mum would come home. She'd have some ideas. And of course I wanted to tell her all about Lorette and the steroids. So much was happening at the moment, I couldn't keep it all in my head. Not that there's much room there at the best of times.

For a moment I sat at my dressing table and stared into space. There was something in the back of my mind that wanted to come to the front. I let it come. And then I wished I hadn't. It went like this: *You've got a perfect excuse for forgetting the date — all that drama about Lorette and the drugs. But his excuse was pathetic: falling asleep over a video! Who's going to believe that? Maybe he just couldn't be bothered to turn up. And if he did fall asleep just before a date with you, well, it's not very flattering, is it?*

The things that turn up in my mind, sometimes! You know, it often seems as though I haven't got any control over my thoughts. Who puts these terrible ideas in my head? Whoever it is, I wish they wouldn't. I heard a key in the lock.

"Jane! I'm home!" Mum called from the hall.

I ran out right away.

"Mum! So much has happened this evening! It's really unbelievable!"

Mum looked great. Her eyes were shining, and she was grinning from ear to ear. For a split second I wondered if she was falling in love with Andy Fowler's dad, and whether they would get married, and if that would make Andy and me brother and sister. Would it mean that we couldn't get married? Not that I was ever going to marry Andy Fowler, of course. I was just interested in a kind of detached way.

Isn't the human brain an incredible thing? I mean, that whole thought, including the wedding of Mum and Andy Fowler's dad at Hackney Registry Office with me looking like Madonna in a short red suit, flashed through my mind in less than a second. There wasn't any time to think about it in detail, now. I'd save it up and get it out to think about again, later. I hadn't even got as far as the wedding that Andy and I weren't going to have, and the dress I wasn't going to wear.

Right now Mum's relationship with Tony Fowler — normally the most fascinating thing I could ever imagine happening — had to take a back seat.

"Mum! You'll never believe it! They had a dope test and Lorette's result was positive! She was disqualified and her mum and dad are in a terrible state. I went round there and Mr Winstone was so mad, he practically jumped down Mike's throat. Although it serves Mike right in a way, I mean as it turned out there was nothing in it, but for a minute I was quite scared — "

"Hey! Hey! Hold your horses!"

Mum sat me down, and refused to listen to any more until she'd made us both a cup of hot chocolate. Then she lay down on the sofa, kicked off her shoes and kind of groaned with relief.

"Now, let's hear it. Start at the beginning and one thing at a time."

So I told her the lot. She listened very carefully, curled up on the sofa, cuddling her mug of hot chocolate, and she didn't interrupt once till I'd finished. Then she said,

"What exactly were these pills Mike gave her? Were they in a packet?"

"No. In an envelope. But I'm sure they were aspirins. They always are."

"I wonder," said Mum, looking at the clock. "No, it's a bit late to ring his mum. I'll ring her tomorrow, just to ask."

"Oh dear," I said, "I hope Mike won't get into trouble."

"Why should he get into trouble?"

"Well, for stealing pills from his mum's medicine cupboard."

"What's he do it for, anyway?"

"Well, he . . . I know it sounds a bit silly . . . " I hesitated. I hoped Mum wouldn't react badly. "But he pretends they're real drugs. I mean, we all know they're not. It's just a sort of . . . game," I finished lamely. Mum was quiet for a while.

"There's something rather sweet and innocent about that," she said eventually. "But there's something a bit frightening about it too. Jane . . . ?"

"Yes?"

"You haven't ever, well . . . had anything to do with real drugs, have you? You can tell me, love — I need to know."

"No, Mum. Never," I said firmly. "I swear it's true. I wouldn't. Honestly. The whole idea scares me stiff."

"Quite right," said Mum. "Good girl. It scares me stiff, too."

We had a quick hug, then. Poor Mum. It must be terrible, being a parent, sometimes.

Then I remembered the other piece of news — that I was going to Larry Payne's tomorrow, for lunch. Mum brightened up at that thought.

"Oh, how nice," she said. "I'm so glad. How nice of him. I wonder what they're like."

"But *Mum* — what shall I wear?"

"Why not your ordinary clothes?"

"Well, I'd rather look a bit, you know — special."

"Of course you would. Let's go and see what we've got."

We went through my whole wardrobe, but we couldn't agree on anything. Then we went through Mum's, and there didn't seem to be anything there either.

"Ah well," said Mum, "too bad. You'll have to go in the nude."

That's what I love about my mum. She says things nobody else's mum would ever say — not in a million years.

We both fell about laughing at the thought of my going to Larry's in the nude.

"I expect his mum would be too polite to make any comment," wheezed Mum, in danger of collapse. "You'd have to be jolly careful not to spill any tea in your lap, though."

"Wait a minute!" I yelled all of a sudden. "What about my new dress? From Wayne — and Lorette," I added, because *from Wayne* sounded a bit . . . you know.

"Where is it?"

"In the laundry basket. I clean forgot. Could we get it washed and dried and everything, in time?"

"Oh yes," said Mum. "We'll hand-wash it and hang it over the bath overnight. You *shall* go to the ball."

Then it was time for bed. I kissed Mum on the cheek and gave her a big hug.

"Hey, Mum!" I said. "I nearly forgot — how was your date?"

Mum crinkled up her nose like a naughty kid.

"Hee, hee!" she said, "wouldn't you like to know?" and slipped away to her bed. I could still hear her laughing to herself now and then after I'd gone to bed and put the light out. Mum seemed to be getting younger and younger at the moment — and I seemed to be getting older and older. It was all very, very odd.

15

What a great Sunday morning that was! Mum had ironed my dress whilst I did the washing up and vacuuming: it was a deal. Then I had a bath and did my hair and spent ages on my face. By the time I'd finished, I almost fancied myself. The love-bite had faded, thank goodness. Mum looked me up and down and smiled.

"You look almost human, Jane," she said. That's her way of saying I look really great — by our standards, anyway. She sprayed a little bit of her spicy perfume on my wrists, kissed me on the brow, and waved me off.

"Have a lovely time!" she called. "Just be yourself and they're sure to like you."

I was quite nervous as I walked along. But the dress danced around my knees again and sort of cheered me up. I wondered how many other girlfriends Larry had invited home, and whether his mum would approve of me or not. It would be important not to say anything silly. That was going to be difficult. Five minutes is about the longest I can go, normally.

It was odd, going right up the path and ringing the doorbell. Two months ago I'd never have dreamed that I'd actually be invited here. It was fantastic. It showed how far I'd come in a few short weeks. From just another anonymous little hero-worshipping fourth former, to official girlfriend, invited to Sunday lunch. I wondered what sort of Sunday lunch it would be, and whether I'd be too nervous to eat.

The door opened and there he stood! Looking even more attractive than usual in a sort of dark green college sweatshirt from some American university. It suited the colour of his skin, made him look tanned and healthy.

"Hey! You look fantastic!" he said, and stood aside for me to come in. As he closed the door behind me, he caught me by the arm and gave me quite a long kiss on the cheek. I wriggled free. I didn't want the rest of his family to see us kissing. It should be private, I reckon.

"Come into the sitting room," he said. "I was just listening to a new cassette. It's Madonna."

"Oh great! I love her."

We went into the sitting room and Larry pulled me down on to the sofa beside him. I sat back and listened. They were good songs, and it was great having Larry's arm round my shoulders. I kept expecting the door to open and somebody else to come in, but I thought his mum would be busy with the lunch and maybe his dad was at the pub or something.

When he was putting the cassette away into its box, Larry suddenly remembered again about last night's news of Lorette and the drugs.

"Oh, Larry! It was awful! We reckon somebody must've sort of doped her without her knowing, like a racehorse sort of thing."

"Well, that's her story and she's sticking to it,"

said Larry with a strange half-smile on his face. I couldn't understand what he found so funny. And I couldn't understand what he said, either.

"What do you mean, that's her story?"

"What sort of drug was it anyway?"

"Steroids."

"Classic," Larry shook his head. He still looked sort of amused. "Honestly. I don't know how they think they can get away with it."

"Who? The people who drugged her?"

"Ah, come on, Jane, grow up. Lorette knows what's what. She's got her head screwed on. Running is her big thing. It's her chance to be a star. I bet there's nothing she wouldn't do for a chance of getting into the British team."

"No, there isn't! She didn't have the faintest idea how she could have had a positive result! Lorette's incredibly health-conscious. She'd never mess about with drugs or anything like that."

"Oh no? How can you be so sure?"

"I know her, that's how! She's my best friend. She's got really high standards, you know, Larry. It's just — well, impossible that she took any stuff like that on purpose."

"Well, you can think what you like, and I'll think what I like."

"No! I don't want you thinking things like that about my friend!"

"Hey, kid — you can't control the way I think. C'mon now. Be reasonable."

"You're the one who's not being reasonable! I know Lorette, Larry. She just wouldn't do this.

This is a real tragedy for her. I want you to be sympathetic, not all horrible and suspicious."

"Look, Jane. I've got to think for myself. I know a bit more about the world than you do. Don't I?"

"Why?"

"Well, I'm older. And I'm a bloke. I know what these West Indians are like, see? Out of their heads on dope, most of them, day and night."

"But that's a complete lie! Lorette's family aren't like that at all. They're totally, well, moral and stuff. Her mum and dad go to church every Sunday. They're ever so religious. And they're so upset about all this. You should have seen them yesterday. Her mum was crying bucketsful."

"Oh yeah, sure. They can turn it on like a tap."

"Larry! Don't talk like that!"

I jumped up off the sofa. I'd forgotten all about his family and I was really shouting. I felt furious. Why couldn't he give me support, back me up on this?

"Don't you tell me how to talk, kid. I say what I think. You should respect that."

"Well, you should respect Lorette!"

"Look, your friend's a great runner. And like most great runners, she's probably a pill-head. A dope fiend. They're all the same, these athletes. And you should hear them bleat about how innocent they are when they get caught. Remember that guy who won the Gold Medal in the Olympics and then got disqualified?"

"But Larry — " My words ran out. I could see I'd never convince him. But I so hated to hear him talk like that about Lorette, I couldn't just stop trying to defend her. I felt my chin begin to wobble. Damn it, I was going to cry!

"Hey! Come on!" Larry jumped up off the sofa, took me in his arms and hugged me. "Don't cry. Cheer up, kid. Sorry if I upset you." Then he gave me a big, slow kiss, and I started to relax a bit. But I still couldn't really concentrate on the kiss. He was being nice to me now, and that made me feel better. But my brain was still busy with its thoughts.

You shouldn't expect Larry to agree with you about everything, it said. *It would be really dull if everybody agreed about everything, wouldn't it? Of course it looks bad that Lorette's test was positive. I bet Larry's not the only person to think the worst. After all, he doesn't really know her, even if he has met her a couple of times. Remember he has a tendency to look on the black side of things.*

All the time I was thinking that, Larry was going on kissing me. I thought maybe it was time for the kiss to come to an end, because surely his mum might come in, so I wriggled free, and smiled at him.

"Sorry," I said. "I just got a bit hot under the collar about Lorette. It'll sort itself out. Can I meet your folks now? Maybe I can give your mum a hand."

"You what?" Larry looked blank.

"Give her a hand. With the lunch or whatever."

A slow grin spread over Larry's face.

"Hey! Did you think my folks were here?"

I was confused.

"Aren't they?"

146

" 'Course not. They've gone to Southend. Coming back tonight. And my brother's with his girlfriend in Bristol." He came up to me and put his arms round my waist. "Why do you think I asked you over?"

I hesitated.

"Well — to meet your folks, I thought."

Larry laughed, and squeezed my waist a little.

"Sorry, kid. That bit comes later. This bit is a lot more fun."

Then he kissed me again.

It was different to be kissing indoors. Usually we'd been outside my front door, kissing goodnight. Or on a bus. This was really strange, knowing that nobody could see us. It was exciting. But in a way it was a bit disturbing, too. I broke free again.

"Can't we have any lunch, then?" I asked playfully. "Aren't you going to feed me?"

"Sure," he said. "Let's go and see what there is."

We had baked beans on toast. I warmed the beans up whilst Larry burnt the toast. It was fun: we laughed a lot. A few beans flew across the kitchen as Larry tried to flick them into my open mouth. I thought how happy I'd be if we could always have a laugh like this. Well, maybe it would get better and better. Maybe things were changing, developing, growing. Larry seemed happy and relaxed today, now that we'd stopped arguing about Lorette.

We washed up together, pretending to be an old couple in their eighties called Harold and Ada.

"There's a bit of tomato sauce on this plate,

Ada," said Larry in a quavery old voice. "I'm going to have to give you a good hiding again for that — if I can find my iron pills."

I laughed so much I had to hold on to the sink. Larry was really great when he got going. He was as funny as Ginger Mike. And much better looking.

After we'd finished putting the things away, Larry yawned and stretched and mussed up my hair a bit. I didn't mind when he did it.

"Hey! Want to see my motorbike magazines?" he asked. "And some photos of me doing motocross?"

Well, the thought of the bike magazines wasn't wildly exciting, but there might be a glamorous pic of Larry in his leathers that I could steal away and pin over my bed.

"OK!" I grinned.

"This way," said Larry. "Follow me up to the den."

We went up to the top of the house, where there was a long low room under the eaves. Larry had to bend down near the window so as not to bump his head on the rafters. It was a nice room. I love attics. They're sort of romantic. Larry had pinned up motorbike posters everywhere and there were a few pictures of naked girls too. I wasn't sure I liked them. But Larry didn't seem too interested in them. He was kissing me again, and holding me very close to his side.

"Come on," he said, "I'll get my albums out and bore you to death."

He threw a couple of photo albums on to the bed, and we sat down and looked at them.

"That's the first Yamaha my brother ever had,"

he said, showing me a picture of a totally ordinary motorbike. Larry's brother was standing beside it. I was much more interested in him. Was he like Larry? It was hard to tell. He was covered from head to foot in motorcycle clothes and wearing a full helmet.

"Is your brother like you?" I asked. Larry grinned and pulled my hair gently.

"Why? You're not going to run off with him, are you?"

"Don't be stupid! Of course not! It's you I — like."

"Ah! I'm glad you — like me. Because I — like you," said Larry, imitating the way I'd hesitated over the word. Then he kind of leaned back on the bed and pulled me down with him. Before I could say anything more, another big kiss was unfolding. I heard both the albums fall on the floor. Larry didn't seem to care. He was really getting involved in this kiss. I must try to, too.

This was a real chance to learn how to kiss. Here we were, with complete privacy and all afternoon ahead of us. I really must get some practice in.

"I don't think I'm very good at kissing yet," I said when he finally surfaced. It was a bit hard to hold a conversation with him, though — he'd disappeared round the back of my neck.

"All you need is lots and lots of practice," he rumbled from somewhere behind my ear. Then he came back round the front and kissed me again. I closed my eyes and tried to let go, to stop my mind from working. But all sorts of strange thoughts came into my head.

There are some girls, said my brain — it was really irritating me, the way it kept butting in — *who don't have normal feelings. They don't enjoy kissing or anything. They're abnormal. You might be one of those.* I opened my eyes. I could see beyond Larry's head, up to the ceiling. There was a picture up there of a girl wearing a black skin-tight leather suit, only it was all unzipped down the front, if you know what I mean. It was embarrassing. I didn't know where to look. I turned my eyes away and saw a large damp stain on the ceiling, shaped like Africa. Oh help! I wasn't concentrating. I was one of those girls. I was that dreaded word: frigid.

Larry wasn't, though. He emerged from his next kiss with a very red face and sort of panting.

"You turn me on!" he whispered. "You turn me on too much!"

And he squeezed parts of me that had never been squeezed before, and they were surprised. I wished we could go back to looking at the motorbike books. Although in theory there was nothing I liked more than being kissed by Larry or told that I turned him on, there was something a bit embarrassing, even frightening, about the whole situation. I felt uneasy.

Now he was off again — burrowing inside my dress. The buttons down the front were old and thin, and the whole dress was a bit fragile. I was afraid he was going to tear it.

"Hey! Steady on!" I said. "Gently does it! Don't ruin my dress."

"Let's take it off, then," he whispered, and his hot breath blasted my eyelashes.

"Oh, no, Larry," I said hurriedly. "I can't do that."

"Let me persuade you," he smiled, and his tongue came out between his lips and sort of flicked all over my face like a snake. Then it settled into another kiss, only this one was a lot more stormy than the other ones and I was beginning to feel seasick. Larry was very strong, and he was starting to do things that I really didn't like. Lying there all afternoon, just talking and kissing, would have been my idea of heaven. But Larry wanted more. And I realised with a blinding flash that I didn't, and somehow I had to stop him. It was going to be like stopping a runaway truck that's hurtling downhill with the brakes broken.

"Larry!" I tried to wriggle free. "Please don't! Stop!"

He didn't answer. He only growled, and sort of bit a handful of my dress, with a handful of me inside it. He was lying on top of me now, and he was so heavy that I couldn't move.

"Stop!" I gasped. "I don't want to do this! Larry! Stop!"

" 'Course you do!" he gasped. "Or why did you come here?"

"But I thought — your folks would be here."

"Well, why did you come up to my den?"

"To see your motorbike photos."

"Don't make me laugh! Motorbikes bore you stiff. I know why you came up here and so do you. Now let's get on with it."

And he sort of dived into my face with his mouth open. I had to fight. There was no other way out. I struggled desperately, but he had hold of both my wrists and he was incredibly strong. The skin on my wrists burned in protest.

"Stop it, Larry, I want to go home!" I shouted.

"Nobody can hear you. Come on, Jane. You know you want to really."

"I do not!"

Now he was biting my neck.

"Stop it! I hate that!" I yelled. But he didn't stop. He was sort of laughing to himself all the time, too. I felt a sudden surge of fury, and I remembered what Wayne had said about defending myself. Suddenly I got cunning. I went limp. I even smiled. Larry noticed and was still for a minute.

"Turn over on your side, then," I said. "You're squashing me."

As he turned, I let him have it. Where it hurts.

Then I was off that bed in a flash and out of the door. I didn't stop to look back — I just knew he wouldn't be able to chase me from the noises he was making. I hoped I hadn't killed him. Altogether, I mean. After the way he'd behaved, I wouldn't have minded killing him just a little.

I ran down the stairs and out into the street, slamming the front door behind me. Then I ran all the way to the railway station and beyond it before I slowed down. Finally I remembered to do up the front of my dress. Thank goodness I hadn't met anybody. Hot tears of shame and rage were flooding down my cheeks. But I couldn't go home. I couldn't let Mum see me like this. Lorette's house was just two streets away. I started to run again, desperate for a friendly face.

My lungs were almost bursting when I got there. I rang the doorbell and leaned against the porch, panting, till somebody came. The door opened and there stood Wayne.

"Jane!" he gasped. "What . . . ?"

I just fell into his arms. I couldn't help it.

16

Lorette appeared in the hall and for a few minutes I just hugged them both and cried and cried like a baby. I felt as if I'd burst. It was such a relief to see them. Then they helped me into their sitting room and gave me a cup of tea and the whole story came flooding out. Luckily Mr and Mrs Winstone were out at a meeting, or I'd have been completely tongue-tied. Lorette had her arm round me all the time and I knew how lucky I was to have such a good friend. It was odd: just a few hours earlier it had been Lorette's mum who was sobbing her heart out, and now it was me.

"I'm goin' to get that guy!" said Wayne, punching the arm of the sofa.

"Oh no, please, Wayne — " I didn't want any trouble. "It was my fault."

"Your fault!" exploded Lorette. "Don't talk like that, Jane! Don't even think like that! Larry Payne is just a menace, that's what! He ought to be locked up!"

"Oh I don't think so. I mean, well, I think he thought I — I mean, I thought I was going to meet his folks, or I'd never . . . "

"Yeah, yeah," said Wayne. "It's not your fault, Jane. You promise not to think like that, now. No guilty feelings, OK?"

"That's right!" said Lorette. "You're a victim,

see? Larry's a typical hard nut. Male violence. That's all he understands."

"Well, he was all right while we were having lunch," I said, pathetically still trying to defend him. "It was only after we — "

"Look at those marks on your wrists!" Wayne took my hand in his long brown fingers and gently stroked the bruise marks where Larry had held me tight. "Don't say anything in defence of this guy, Jane. He's just a pig. You gotta face the fact that he wanted to hurt you, and he didn't care about how you felt, at all."

I was silent. They were right. I felt a fool — a miserable fool, for being taken in by him. I thought of all the things Larry had said about Lorette — how she was a bad influence on me, how she was such an ambitious athlete, she was probably a pill-head — and how I'd barely stood up for her. It was this girl who, right now, at the worst moment of her life, was unselfish enough, and loyal enough, to stand up for me.

"You're right," I said weakly. "I don't want to talk about it any more." I tried to smooth the horrible crumples on the skirt of my dress. One of the buttons had been torn off.

"I'll get you a safety pin for that," said Lorette, seeing me fiddling with the snapped threads. She went upstairs.

"The dress is fantastic, Jane," said Wayne.

"He nearly bloody ruined it," I sniffed.

"Don't think any more about him, now. That guy is really bad news."

"How's — Lorette?" I whispered. I was a little

afraid to mention the drugs business whilst she was in the room.

"She's much better today," said Wayne. "She's going to fight and fight to clear her name, she says, no matter if it takes the rest of her life."

"I'll help her," I said, clenching my teeth at the thought of the people who would like to do her down. "I'm going to fight for her."

"Hey, little hedgehog! You look like you're gonna bite!"

Wayne grinned and ruffled my hair.

"If I knew who did this to Lorette, I would bite!" I said. "I'd bite their heads off."

"Fight dem back!" Wayne put on a reggae voice. "Hey! Want to listen to some Bob Marley? Soon make you feel better."

"Oh yes, please, Wayne!"

So when Lorette came back with the safety pin, we all listened to Bob Marley's "Kaya". One of the best albums of all time. So Wayne says, anyway. Real relaxed cool stuff, with the drums and the guitars kind of swaying on the wind and echoing far, as if the music was coming washing to you from thousands of miles away across the ocean. By the end of side one, I was soothed and smoothed and all my tremblings and jangled nerve-endings were washed away in the tides of sound. By the beginning of side two we were all dancing, and we were still dancing when Lorette's mum and dad came home.

"Hello, Jane," said Mrs Winstone. "We were really touched that your mother rang up today to ask if there was anything she could do to help."

"People like your ma, they've got hearts of gold," said Mr Winstone, taking off his jacket. "Others we won't talk about."

And he went out into his garden to see how the tomato plants were doing. I hoped Lorette wouldn't say anything about what had happened between me and Larry, and she didn't. She's got this amazing tact, Lorette. She never opens her mouth except to say something really sensible. Whereas I — well, you know me by now, well enough to realise that if there's something stupid to be said I can be relied upon to say it.

When I got home later that evening, I had to face Mum. I knew she'd be curious to know what had happened. But my heart was beating fast as I walked up the steps. Mum and I had had practically no secrets from each other, ever. But I was really worried about telling her about this. She'd be absolutely furious, of course. She might ring Larry's parents — anything. And she certainly wouldn't let me have so much freedom with boys in the future. I could see her following me on dates at a discreet distance, with the collar of her mac pulled up like a private eye. And maybe Andy Fowler's dad hovering in the background as bodyguard. That wouldn't do a lot for my social life.

So it had to be lies. White lies. It was to protect her. Interesting. All the time I was a little kid, my fibs had been to protect me — from her getting angry at me. Now I was growing up, I had to skirt round the truth for her sake, too. Mind you, I still somehow felt guilty and ashamed about the whole thing, as if it had been my fault somehow. And

I definitely didn't want her to go all silent and disapproving. Here I was at the door. And I still hadn't worked out what to say.

There she was, sitting in a patch of sunlight and cleaning the shoes. She likes doing those cosy sorts of jobs on Sunday evening — after tea the serious business of getting ready for Monday really starts. She looked up as I came in, and I managed to squeeze a brave smile out.

"How did it go, then, love?"

"Oh, it was all a big fuss about nothing. His folks weren't even there," I said, trying to sound casual and flopping down on the sofa.

"What! Do you mean you didn't meet his mum and dad?"

"No. They were away in Southend. His brother was there, though," I added quickly.

"Well, how disappointing. I've been wondering all afternoon how you were getting on, too. What was his brother like?"

"Well, he's a motorbike fanatic." That much I knew. "He's taller than Larry and not quite so good-looking."

I hoped that would be enough information about Larry's brother. I didn't think I could invent much more.

"So what did you do all afternoon?"

"Well, we had some lunch. Beans on toast. And then we looked at some pictures of motorbikes."

"My God! It sounds boring."

I lay down on the sofa, trying to look relaxed. "Well, actually, Mum — it was. I've decided

Larry's a bit of a drag. So I left early and went to see Lorette and Wayne."

"You what? Do you mean you're going off him?"

Mum put down the shoe brush and sat bolt upright, trying hard to fight off a smile.

"More or less. Yes."

"Jane! You clever old thing! You managed to see through him! I am pleased with you, love!"

Mum hurtled out of her chair and gave me a big hug. I felt a total fraud. If there was one thing I hadn't done it was see through him. I'd let him string me right along — almost until it was too late.

"Didn't you ever like him, then, Mum?"

"I'm afraid not. He's the sort of chap I can't stand. Vain, and arrogant, and unfriendly. As for his precious motorbikes — I'd ban the lot of them tomorrow if I was Prime Minister."

I often think it's a good job Mum hasn't got a hope of becoming Prime Minister. She was certainly being a bit hard on motorbikes. I'd tried my best to get interested in them recently, and banning them outright might be going a bit far, I thought. But then, Mum would ban so many things: plastic throw-away bottles, pin-up magazines, and the woman in the library who always looks at us over the top of her glasses.

But was this really what she'd thought about Larry? Vain, arrogant, and unfriendly? I felt sick.

"Wasn't there anything nice about him, then?"

"Well, you must know that better than I do. After all, you went out with him several times."

"He was good-looking."

"Not to my taste, Jane. I don't like handsome men. They're usually terribly pleased with themselves and can't understand it if a girl doesn't want to throw herself at them. I think Andy Fowler's a thousand times more attractive."

A spear of feeling went through me. I got up off the sofa and went over to the window. I wasn't sure why at first but then I realised it was to hide my face from Mum. Not that she was looking. She'd gone back to her shoe polishing.

I sighed, and the sigh made a fog on the windowpane. Beyond it were the trees of the park. I drew a broken heart in the fog. Then I wiped it out. I breathed again. Then I drew a whole heart, healed. But my own heart wasn't back in one piece yet. It was held together with bits of sticky tape and fraying string. Because there was more to be upset about than Larry Payne. I rested my head against the hard glass. A motorbike roared past in the street, and screamed to a halt up at the junction at the top, by the pub. I looked out into the green and waited for the noise to stop.

Back in my own room, I felt relieved. It was odd to lie on my bed and say to myself, *Thank goodness that's over*. There were so many things I didn't have to worry about any more. I didn't have to think what to wear for a date, or whether my spikes were standing up properly. I wouldn't have the problem of not wanting to eat. In fact, right now my stomach was rumbling like a ten-ton truck. And the whole business about saying the right thing had just disappeared out of my life. I didn't have to worry about not offending Larry, or not irritating him, or not boring him. I could be as boring as I blinking well liked!

"Hee, hee!" I thought, and hugged myself and waved my legs in the air. Freedom! I could slop around in my jeans once again. And hang around in the cemetery with the gang. And enjoy Ginger Mike's craziness without having to try and explain it to anybody. I felt really comfortable and warm, back in my old life. And when Mum called me in to supper and placed a steaming plate of scrambled eggs in front of me, I felt as if I'd woken up out of a nightmare.

I just hadn't realised what a strain it was, going out with Larry until it stopped.

"You know, Mum," I said, through mouthfuls of egg, "I feel so relieved now I'm not going out with him any more. And I was so thrilled when he first asked me out. Isn't it weird?"

"I felt like that when your dad left," said Mum. Immediately I pricked up my ears. Mum didn't talk about Dad very much, and I'd been so much younger when he moved out, my memories of what he'd been like were very dim.

"What . . . what was he like? To live with, I mean?"

Mum buttered a piece of toast and smiled to herself.

"It's amazing, now, to think of what I put up with," she said. "We were both working, right from the time you were at school. Well, we had to. He didn't earn enough to keep us, but together we could just about manage. But guess who had to do all the cooking, and cleaning, and shopping?"

"You!"

"Got it in one. When he got home from work, he just slumped in front of the telly waiting for me to get him his supper. I was practically dead on my feet — I was a waitress in those days, that's before I got onto reception — and I was so dead-beat one day I actually fainted in the bathroom."

"You didn't, did you, Mum? How awful!"

"Yes. You were playing on the sitting room floor with your dolls, and he was watching the football. I felt a bit odd so I went into the bathroom and then my head sort of buzzed and everything went black. When I came to, I remember seeing the loo from below. It was so strange. I couldn't think what it was at first, or where I was. For a minute I thought I must've had an accident and I must be in a hospital. Then I realised I was on the bathroom floor.

"I sat up slowly and had a few sips of water, and put my head between my knees. Then when my head cleared, I managed to stagger down into the sitting room and collapse on the sofa. And do you know what he said? He didn't even stop watching the telly. He just said, 'Where the hell's that tea? What have you been playing at? You can't lounge about like a lady of leisure, my girl.' "

"Did you belt him?"

"I was sorely tempted. But I knew it would be dangerous. Besides, I didn't have any strength. Still, at that moment I knew I'd had enough. It was the end. Either he had to go or I did."

"Did you have rows about it?"

"I just went on strike. I said, 'Look here, Dave. I'm doing twice as much work as you are. I earn good money all day and then I come home and you expect me to wait on you hand and foot. Well, I've had enough.' "

"What did he say?"

"He said, 'Don't give me any of that Women's Lib crap. Looking after the family and the home is woman's work. You won't get me poncing around in an apron like some daft buggers. Need their heads examining.' Then I said, 'Well, I think I need my head examining for being at your beck and call all these years. If you want to stay here you'll have to do your bit, shopping and cooking and cleaning. It's not woman's work. It's work for all of us.' "

I was speechless at the thought of Mum standing up to him like that. It sounded so incredibly brave.

"Then what happened?"

"Well, I stopped cooking and shopping and cleaning. I gave you your supper and I just had bread and cheese myself. After a few days he stopped coming home in the evenings. He'd stay on at the pub, boozing. Then one night he came home and packed his bag. He said he'd met somebody who really loved him and knew how to take care of a man. A willing slave, in other words."

"Weren't you upset?"

"Not likely. It was marvellous. I had the flat to myself, my time to myself, I could do what I liked, and I didn't have to make excuses for things or ask permission from anybody."

"But wasn't he nice once? I mean, when you first knew him?"

"Charming, he was. Pampered me. Took me out, bought me presents, all the usual things. Swept me off my feet. We got married six weeks after we met. I must've been off my rocker. Well, you know what they say. Marry in haste, repent at leisure."

I knew what she meant. A brief image of being married to Larry Payne flashed across my brain, and it made me shudder.

"But — after he'd gone — didn't you get lonely?"

"Eventually."

Silence fell, and Mum toyed with her spoon. I waited. I felt more was coming. Mum stared out of the window. She looked as if she was in a trance. But she said nothing.

"Mum . . . ? What about Andy Fowler's dad? Are you in love with him?"

Mum turned to me and her eyes were strangely shiny.

"I don't know, love," she said quietly. "It's been years since I've been out with anybody. And he's very different from your dad. He's brought Andy up on his own, so he's very handy around the house. And he sort of . . . seems to want to take care of me, instead of wanting me to take care of him."

"Will you marry him?"

"Hey, steady on! We've only been seeing each other for a short while! I tell you something, Jane. Nothing in the world's going to make me rush into living with a man again."

"Not even a nice one like Tony Fowler?"

Mum grinned.

"Well. Let's wait and see. Gently does it. I've got all the time in the world."

I sighed. I wished my dad had taken care of Mum properly. I felt a bit guilty about him being such a lazy pig. But it wasn't my fault. There was nothing I could do. Except make up for him.

I kissed her on the head and told her to watch TV. Then I cleared the table, washed up, dried up, put the dishes away, scrubbed the kitchen floor, cleaned the oven, and cleared out the fridge. I found some jars of gherkins in there that had grown long grey beards. It made them look like grandpa gherkins.

"Jane," Mum's head came round the kitchen door, "are you trying to prove something?"

"I'm making up for Dad," I grinned.

"You soppy old thing," Mum said. "Stop it now. You've earned your gold star."

I obeyed. I'd really enjoyed all that cleaning. It had somehow helped me to get Larry out of my system. Now Mum and I were two single girls, happy to be on our own, thanks very much, and we'd never be taken in again by useless, lazy, vain or violent men. From now on, everything would be under control. Just as I was getting up off my knees, the phone rang.

"Hello?" Mum answered it. "It's for you. It's Ginger Mike."

How odd of him to phone at this time in the evening. I grabbed the receiver.

"Hello?"

165

"Jane! This is Mike! Listen, something terrible's happened! Wayne was in a fight with Larry Payne and he got stabbed. He's in hospital. The ambulance came. I saw it. There was blood all over his shirt."

17

My first impulse was to rush out and run all the way to the hospital. But Mum grabbed my arm and talked some sense into me.

"What hospital?" she asked. "We don't even know. It's terribly late. Look, let me ring Mrs Winstone and ask how he is."

So Mum rang. There was no answer. Of course — they were all at the hospital. At Wayne's death bed. I burst into tears.

"Stop it, Jane," said Mum firmly. "Don't panic. We'll ring round the hospitals. Pull yourself together and make us a cup of cocoa."

I did, and by the time it was ready, Mum had managed to contact the right hospital.

"Wayne is OK," said Mum firmly, looking calm and rather stern. "He's not in danger. They're just keeping him in overnight for observation."

I burst into tears again — tears of relief, this time.

"It was Larry," I sobbed. "He was in a fight with Larry."

"What? How come?" Mum was amazed.

I realised that there wasn't much more I could tell her without confessing my part in it all. I might have known Wayne would go off and be all silly and heroic. He'd said he was my friend and body-guard often enough. He'd even threatened to get

Larry if he ever did anything to hurt me. But it's no use being heroic if the other guy has a knife.

"Oh, do stop that whining," said Mum irritably. She was a bit on edge, since Mike's phone call. Anything to do with violence always makes her — well, violent. Whenever there's a terrorist bomb and people get blown to bits, Mum grinds her teeth and tells me what she'd do with the terrorists if she could get her hands on them. It's mostly to do with the food processor. She's never laid a finger on me, though.

"Sometimes," she says, shaking her fist at me, "I think that's where I went so horribly wrong."

Tonight I reckoned it was time I went to bed. I left Mum staring moodily into space. I hoped she wouldn't stay up too late. But I heard her moving about and clearing up a few minutes later. I curled up and switched out my light. But I knew I wasn't going to sleep for hours.

When I finally did manage to get off, I had the most horrendous dreams. Larry was coming at me out of a dark alley with a knife, then he put me in a sack and I couldn't get out and I struggled and screamed and was suffocating, then woke up whimpering and panting in the dark. But that was nothing to the next dream.

In that one, Larry cut Wayne up into little bits and I had to put him together again, like a jigsaw puzzle. Only it wasn't bits of body — it was bits of a picture of Wayne. I knew I had to solve the puzzle by a certain time or Wayne would be dead for ever. Then Larry came in and held my wrists very tight, so I dropped all the jigsaw pieces on the floor. Then I woke up, lying on my crossed wrists. My hands had gone all numb. By then it was nearly time to get up. I didn't dare to go to sleep again after that lot. I was exhausted.

Lorette wasn't at the bus stop. This was terrible. I'd been relying on her to tell me how Wayne was. Maybe she was in hospital by Wayne's bedside. Maybe he'd taken a turn for the worse. Maybe Mum had been lying to me last night! Maybe Wayne was really dead — and Mum couldn't face telling me! That was why she'd been so quiet and on edge. Yes! It all made sense! I almost fainted at the thought. Luckily Sudeshna got on at the next stop, with Ginger Mike.

"Hey!" said Mike. "Did you ring the hospital last night?"

"Yes. Mum did. They said he was OK but they were keeping him in for observation."

"Keeping who in?" asked Sudeshna with a frown. Of course, she didn't know anything about it.

"Larry Payne stabbed Wayne last night," said Ginger Mike. "It was all because of Jane."

"No it was not!" I gasped in horror. "You mustn't say that, Mike."

"I was there!" said Mike in an unnecessarily loud voice. "Larry and his mates were sitting around outside the pub, drinking. I was going up and down the road on my skates. I saw the whole thing."

"What happened?" asked Sudeshna breathlessly.

"Well, Wayne came down the street and went straight up to Larry and sort of grabbed him by the shirt." My heart missed a beat. I couldn't bear to listen, but I couldn't bear not to, either. "He

169

said, *Listen, Larry Payne, you hurt a friend of mine today*. And Larry sort of looked blank and said, *What the hell are you on about?* And Wayne pushed him up against the wall and said, *You know who I mean. You didn't give her a chance. She came round our house, dress all torn, bruises all over her, crying her eyes out*. And then Larry sort of pushed him off and said, *Huh! If it's that little scrubber Jane Watts you're talking about, you're wasting your time. She led me on. Little tart. Begging for it, she was. Then she goes all coy at the last minute. Next time she'll get what she deserves*.

By now my face was scarlet. I was sure the whole busload of passengers was listening. You could almost see their ears flapping.

"Please, Mike!" I whispered. "For goodness" sake — shut up! Wait till we're at school!"

"But how did the fight actually start?" asked Sudeshna. For somebody so gentle, she seemed to be a bit too interested in all the gory details.

"Well, when Larry said that, Wayne just hit him. Smack on the nose. Then there was a bit of a scuffle, and one or two of Larry's mates crowded round. There was some shouting — I couldn't see what was happening. Then they all suddenly ran off, and Wayne was sort of kneeling on the pavement holding his chest."

"Oh, my God!" I felt sick.

"I went straight into the pub, and told them to ring for an ambulance," said Ginger Mike. "With my roller-skates still on."

"But what about Wayne?"

"There was this woman out walking her dog,

and she was a nurse. She took care of him till the police and ambulance came. Then the police interviewed me," said Ginger Mike proudly. "I made a statement. They wrote it all down."

"But how was Wayne whilst you were waiting for the ambulance?" asked Sudeshna.

"He didn't say much. There was blood all over his shirt."

Sudeshna gave a little scream, and I felt faint again.

"Oh God!" said Sudeshna. "I hope he won't die."

And we all, in our different ways, secretly added Amen to that.

Larry wasn't at school, nor, of course, were Lorette and Wayne. But the whole place was buzzing with rumours. I got some strange looks in the yard. But Sudeshna and Ginger Mike stuck close by my side, and Mike was rabbiting on about the latest Douglas Adams book, so I had something else to think about instead of Wayne's bloodstained shirt. Still, I didn't like all the eyes looking my way. I began to feel paranoid. It was almost a relief to get into the Maths lesson.

After school, I ran to the nearest phone box and rang Lorette's number.

"Come on over," said Lorette. "Wayne's home now and he really wants to see you."

I ran all the way to their house. In fact, I think I did myself an injury. By the time I got there my knees had definitely turned into taramasalata and I was panting so hard I couldn't speak. Lorette opened the door and gave me rather a hard look.

I cringed — insofar as you can cringe, if you're panting like a sheepdog who's just run over two mountains. I hoped she wasn't going to blame me for all this. But who wouldn't blame me? Those words that Larry had said about me burned into my memory. Were they true? I couldn't bear to think about it.

Wayne was sort of reclining on the sofa. His chest was strapped up. I paused by his side. I wanted to hug him but I thought in his present state it might kill him.

"Oh Wayne," I sort of squeaked. "You are an idiot!"

Then a huge tear bounced out of my right eye and ran down my nose. Wayne raised his hand. I squeezed it. Then I sort of fell at his feet. I grabbed his feet and hugged them with all my might.

"Hey, little hedgehog!" he said. "Watch out! My ma says those socks are worse than toxic waste!"

Dear old Wayne. Joking already.

"How's — how's the wound?" I asked, feeling a bit dizzy. It was just as well I was already on the floor. If I did actually faint, it wouldn't be far to slump.

"Fine," said Wayne with a grin. "It was a really neat bit of knife-work. Missed the heart, missed the lung, missed the liver. It landed smack in the middle of nothing particularly important. Man, if you're goin" to get stabbed, it couldn't have happened in a more convenient place."

"Still hurts like hell, though," said Lorette. "Don't it, Wayne? The doctors say he's gotta rest for two, maybe three weeks."

"They said I'll heal easy, though," said Wayne. " 'Cos I'm so young and strong and gorgeous."

"There was this real sexy nurse there," said Lorette. "She really fancied Wayne."

"C'mon, sister! She was just kidding," grinned her brother, looking quite pleased all the same. Then they both suddenly looked at me, sort of in unison. I stammered.

"I — I — couldn't believe it when I heard," I said. "Look, Wayne, I'll never be able to . . ." Damn it, my mouth was trembling and more tears were lining up, waiting their turn down the ski-jump of my nose. "To forgive myself. I should never have mentioned — "

"Listen!" yelled Wayne, a little too loud for his own comfort. "Ouch — No, listen, Jane. I told you, I'm your bodyguard. I couldn't stand to think how that guy had treated you, and when I went up to him I couldn't stand the way he talked about you either. I hit him and it felt great. If he hadn't had two friends with him I'd have given him a hiding."

"Don't talk about it now," said Lorette. "Come to the kitchen with me, Jane. I'm gonna make a cup of tea. My mum'll be home soon. And Wayne's gotta take it easy. Relax for five minutes, you crazy thing!"

"Leave Jane here," said Wayne. "I want to talk to her."

"No. You'd get too excited," scolded Lorette. "You just relax now for five minutes like that nurse said. We'll be back in a minute."

I followed Lorette to the kitchen and watched

whilst she put the kettle on. I'd got the feeling I was due for a big talking-to. And I was right.

"So. I hope you've realised by now who's a decent guy and who isn't, Jane Watts," she said, banging the cupboard doors as she got the tea out.

"Yes. Well. It's obvious." I hung my head. "I completely misjudged Larry. He totally took me in. I was dazzled by his looks and his reputation and all that. Nobody's going to take me in like that again."

"He's going to go on saying bad things about you, too," said Lorette grimly. "And some people's goin' to believe him."

I writhed. I got the feeling she wanted me to writhe, too. She blamed me for her brother getting hurt. And why not? Suppose the knife had been an inch further to the right? Suppose Wayne had been lying in a mortuary now, instead of on a sofa in the next room? What would she be thinking of me, then? I started to cry again.

"It's no use worrying about that," she said. "He'll say what he'll say. You just have to trust the people you know and like to be loyal to you. They won't take no notice of what he says."

"I wasn't crying about that," I sniffed. "I was crying about — what it would have been like if — Wayne had got killed."

"Yeah," said Lorette, getting out the cups. "I thought a lot about that, too. You know, Jane — " she faced me squarely and looked right into my eyes, "Wayne would never have gotten into this mess if he hadn't been crazy about you."

I cringed. This I didn't want to hear. I opened

my mouth, but no sounds came out. So I closed it again.

"He's been crazy about you for months," said Lorette. "He don't show his feelings too much, but I can tell. When you started going out with Larry, it really broke him up. He'd kill for you, Jane."

"I — hope not." It sounded pathetic.

"Now listen. You got Larry Payne out of your system, right?"

"Well — it'll take a bit of time to, sort of calm down after all this." I felt flustered. I sensed what Lorette was driving at. I couldn't face all this.

"Listen. Wayne got hurt for you. Right? Well, can't you just be a little bit nicer to him, Jane?"

I panicked. What was she asking me to do? Feel things for Wayne that I just couldn't?

"I — I do love him," I whispered. "As a brother."

"Stuff that! He's got me to love him as a brother. All he wants from you is a little extra-special tenderness."

I sighed and shrugged. This was unfair. I did love Wayne — deeply and thoroughly. But I didn't feel for him the things I'd felt for . . . other people. He didn't light my fire. I only wished he did. How convenient it would be. Lorette my best friend, and her brother my boyfriend. It would make a great team. Together we'd conquer the world or rather, save it. But I couldn't, I just couldn't feel like that about him.

How could I explain to Lorette, though? She was waiting, now, for some sort of word from me. Some sign. I shook my head. I couldn't tell her why I didn't feel like that about Wayne. She was the very last person in the world I could tell. It had to stay a mystery for ever.

The kettle came to the boil, and the front door-bell rang. Lorette switched the kettle off.

"Answer the door will you, Jane?" she said. "I'll just make the tea."

I went to the front door and opened it. There, on the step, with a big bunch of flowers and an enormous bag of grapes, stood Andy Fowler. And every little part of me fizzed, popped, and went up in the air in a secret, invisible firework display, at the sight of him.

18

Well, Andy came in and gave Wayne his grapes and handed the bunch of flowers to Lorette, who kissed him on the cheek. He hugged her and then sat down to talk to Wayne. I followed Lorette into the kitchen and helped her put the flowers in water.

"Hand me down that vase, Jane," she said, unwrapping the bouquet. My hands were shaking so badly, I was afraid I might drop it.

"Wasn't that nice of Andy to — bring these?" I said, trying to sound bright and breezy but only managing to be empty and trembly. Luckily Lorette didn't notice.

"He's just fantastic," she said, plunging the flowers into the vase and shaking them out so they looked right. "Honestly, Jane . . . " she looked at me very seriously, even for Lorette. "If it hadn't been for you I'd never really have got to know him properly. And he's been terrific about the drugs test thing. He's with me all the way. He says he'll stand up for me and do anything he can to help me clear it up."

"So will I!" I said, but it sounded a bit pathetic.

"Yeah," said Lorette, smelling the flowers. There were some freesias among them, and the scent was sweet and strong. "I don't know what I'd have done without him on Saturday. My folks, you know, were really out of control. If it hadn't been for Andy, well, I think we'd have had a family nervous breakdown."

"Is he . . . are you . . . ?" I hovered at the edge of the question I most wanted to ask. "Are you . . . er, sort of, going out together, type thing?"

Lorette smiled to herself, and her eyes shone. She picked up the vase of flowers to carry it to the sitting room.

"Well, we don't have much time to actually go out," she said. "What with my training and everything. And homework. We more sort of . . . stay in together, if you know what I mean." And she gave me a naughty little grin — very unusual for Lorette — and went off to the sitting room.

I tried to follow, but it was hard to get my legs to obey orders. They just sort of stood there, stuck to the floor. I told them to cut it out and get walking. But they knew that through there in the sitting room, I'd have to watch Lorette and Andy being happy together and it was going to be a bit, well, difficult.

Wayne helped. He was on amazing form, considering how badly he'd been injured. Andy made him laugh a lot and Wayne told him to leave off, as it hurt to laugh and if he wasn't careful he'd be back in intensive care. When Andy asked him how it had happened, Wayne gave me a quick look and just said that he'd got mixed up in a fight outside a pub and though Larry Payne was one of the blokes, it was one of the others who'd stabbed him. Not Larry.

I wondered if this was true. Was Wayne just lying so I wouldn't be too upset? Or had it really not been Larry? I desperately wanted it not to have been him. Then at least I wouldn't feel so guilty, so responsible, for Wayne being hurt. I looked hard at Wayne's face, as he shrugged it all off. He gave me another quick look. He was certainly trying to keep all mention of me out of it. I was grateful. Dear old Wayne. If only I could . . . but I couldn't. And the reason was sitting right next to him, with his arm round Lorette. Andy Fowler.

Eventually, after we'd all had too much tea and lots of grapes, Andy stood up and said he'd got to go and cook some spaghetti for his dad's dinner.

"He hasn't trained Jane's mum to wait on him hand and foot, yet," he grinned. "You coming home now, Jane?"

"Yes," I faltered. I supposed I was. I'd been there long enough and Wayne looked tired. I was dreading the walk home with Andy, but knowing him, he would fill in all the silences with a stream of jokes and never even notice how confused I was. The most important thing in the world, now, was to hide what I felt about him. Now I'd admitted it to myself, everything else had become clear.

No wonder I hadn't really got the hang of being kissed by Larry. It wasn't Larry I was interested in, at all. No wonder I'd felt so strange when I'd realised that something special was happening between Lorette and Andy. No wonder I couldn't get excited about dear old Wayne. The person who really turned my spine to water was right here beside me: kissing his girlfriend goodbye.

Lorette waved us off and we set off down her front path. Andy opened the gate for me and somehow it was a bit tricky, getting through it. Not that I was fat any more. I was just totally unco-ordinated. Still, here we were out on the pavement. All I had to do now was put one foot in front of the other till I got to the end of the street. It was only a ten-minute walk. Andy would do the talking. I'd just have to nod occasionally and say yes or no. It may sound like a piece of cake to you, but to me it was about as easy as going up Everest without oxygen.

We set off, and I waited for Andy to say something. But he didn't. I looked hard at the pavement. Small flowers like daisies were pushing their way through the cracks. You could tell that underneath this city street was a meadow. All it needed was a few years left undisturbed, and Nature would take over again. Young trees would come cracking through the stones. Fifty years and it'd be a forest again. What weird thoughts.

Andy was still silent. I couldn't bear it. I didn't dare to look at him. My heart felt full and heavy. I could hardly drag myself along. I'd have given anything to be alone. The silence itself seemed to be hanging on us, weighing us down. Then he spoke.

"Let's have a cup of coffee at Dino's," he said, Dino's was a little bar up ahead — the first one we came to in Church Street.

"Oh yes — that would be nice," I agreed, like an idiot. What I should have said was, *No, thanks, I've got to go*. And zoomed off over the horizon hoping our paths would never cross again. But I'd said yes, so I had to follow him into Dino's. I sat down whilst he got the coffees. Nobody else was there, and Dino was just drying up some glasses with a sad look on his handsome Italian face. The coffee machine made a deafening noise, and there was a TV set throbbing away in the background. I was glad it was noisy. Our silence had come in with us but it wasn't so noticeable in here.

Andy brought the coffee to the table and sat down opposite me. Then he looked me straight into my eyes. I felt I'd been shot. I propped up my head on my hands but it was only a matter of time before my entire body fell apart. One more look from him would do it. I looked down at my coffee instead, and stirred it, but then it swirled around so madly, I felt my head swim. So I looked away past his eyes, over his shoulder, at a poster advertising a rock concert.

"I was sorry to hear about what happened with Larry Payne," said Andy. I had to look at him, then. But only briefly.

"Well, it was never any good really."

"No? I thought you were crazy about him. He was certainly crazy about you."

"No," I stared out of the window, across the street. "Not really. I may have thought I was, but I wasn't. And he certainly didn't give a damn about me."

"Well, he's mad, then," said Andy, and his voice shook a little. I didn't dare look at him. I looked across the street. An old man was wheeling his bike along the pavement. There was a string bag hanging from the handlebars with potatoes in it, and a cat sitting in the bicycle basket. *I'll never forget that old man as long as I live*, I thought.

"Hey," said Andy. "Look at me. Go on. Force yourself."

He was grinning. I could hear it in his voice. I had to look. But as I turned my face to look into his, my stupid chin started juddering like a jelly. Andy's grin faded. There was a look in his eyes I'd never seen before. I wasn't sure what it was. But it seemed to paralyse me, so I just gazed into his eyes and felt myself slipping away and drowning. Two big tears burst out of my eyes and slid down my cheeks.

"Come on, now," said Andy. "It isn't the end of the world."

I blew my nose. I knew it was red by now. In fact, I looked awful. But what did it matter anyway?

"I know it's not the end of the world," I said, sort of blowing a bubble of spit as I spoke.

"You'll get over him," said Andy.

"Oh, bugger *him*!" I burst out. "It's not him I'm upset about."

And then Andy's eyes changed again, and became more serious than I'd ever seen them. And more gentle.

"I know," he said.

That moment I knew he knew what I was thinking. Every little bit. But what was *he* thinking? I couldn't say anything else. Not a word. I was spent. He was going to have to say something to get us out of this mess.

"I'm sorry," he said softly, after a while. "It was

182

bad timing. I . . . " Then he stopped and looked away for a minute. I prayed for him to go on. "You knew I was mad about you, Jane."

My mouth dropped open. I couldn't believe it. This, from Andy Fowler! I couldn't speak. I just gave a little squeak of astonishment.

"I've always been mad about you. But you never seemed interested."

More tears were coming, now. In fact, I was beginning to wish I'd been born with windscreen wipers.

"I didn't realise . . . " I couldn't finish what I had to say. "Anyway Lorette . . . "

"Never mind Lorette for a minute. Just let me have my say. I reckoned I didn't have a chance with you. Then that day in the park . . . up you walked holding Larry Payne's hand. Lorette told me you'd been crazy about him for ages. So I thought, *That's it then. Forget her, mate.* And then . . . "

"You realised Lorette was gorgeous."

"Yeah," he smiled, half sadly, half assertively. "I realised Lorette was gorgeous."

"So it's hard luck, really, isn't it? If I'd known what I was doing — "

"No ifs!" He caught hold of my hand suddenly, and held it for a minute before letting go. It felt like an electric shock. "No ifs. Promise me, Jane."

"All right. Lorette really needs you now."

"She does. And to tell you the truth, I need her, too."

More tears charged down my cheeks. Where were they all coming from? I hadn't touched my coffee yet, but I was going to need a drink soon to make up for all this crying.

"I must go," I said, but I just sat there. My energy had all drained away.

"Drink your coffee first! I paid a fortune for that."

I tried. It was cold, and not very nice either.

"Listen, Jane. We're both very young. I'm only eighteen. And you're practically still in Pampers."

I laughed and choked and spat a bit of coffee in his eye.

"Sorry!"

"It was a pleasure. Do it again in the other eye this time. Go on!"

"Stop it! This isn't funny."

I didn't want to laugh, although in a way it was nice.

"I tell you something that's absolutely true," said Andy, suddenly dead serious again. "We're all young. We got years and years ahead of us. As long as we eat plenty of fruit. Now, listen to this. Lorette may need me now. But sooner or later she's going to find out that I'm not the guy for her."

"What do you mean?"

"I'm too much of an idiot. Lorette really needs someone serious, like her. I'll irritate her, in the end. I just can't help it."

"But I think you're perfect for her! It's great that you can cheer her up and joke and everything. That's exactly what she needs."

"So you don't think she'll get fed up with me?"

"I wouldn't."

"Ah," said Andy, smiling into my eyes and

wiping a tear from my face, "that's what you think. You'd be throwing the saucepans at me within six weeks. I guarantee."

I tried to smile. He wanted me to be brave.

"So that's it, then," I said, heaving a sigh and wiping my face with a paper napkin. I felt a bit better after that.

"Anything could happen," said Andy. "Remember that. Only right now . . . "

"You have to take care of Lorette," I sniffed.

"Right. And I will."

"We will," I said, getting up. "She's my friend, too, you know."

"Jealous is it now? Blimey."

"To tell you the truth," I said as we walked to the door. "I think I'm jealous of both of you."

He grinned, and gave me a brotherly little hug before we walked out into the street.

The sun was shining and I felt better, although very bruised. I put my shades on to hide my swollen eyes.

"Wayne's mad about you," said Andy. "Give him a break."

"Not you, too!" I grumbled. "For God's sake leave me alone! Everyone's on at me all the time about Wayne."

"Sorry. Look — come into the shop a minute." We'd reached Fowler's Fruit Shop. Andy unlocked the door. I stepped inside. "I want to give you something." He went back into the storehouse and came out a moment later with a brown bag of fruit. They looked odd: sort of purple and crinkly.

"What are they?" I asked. He grinned.

"Passion fruit, love. That's the most passionate thing I can give you for the moment."

I picked up a handful of grapes and squashed them in his face. He spat some pips back at me.

"That's more like it," he said. "No more tears. Shall we be friends?"

I nodded. He offered me his hand. His big, warm, strong hand. My hand felt safe inside it. We shook hands. It felt odd and grown-up, like in a book or a film. More tears wanted to come, then, but they were a different kind. Sort of happy tears.

"Go now," he said. "Or I'll do something I'll regret."

I went out. I didn't look back. Right away, I walked to the park and went round and round the lake several times, crying all the way all the different sorts of tears that had been lining up behind my face. Then when my eyes were quite empty, I went into the girls' loos and washed my face. It was over.

19

A couple of days later I went round to Ginger Mike's. I had to take back a few LPs I'd borrowed and Mum kept nagging at me to return them. It was early evening, and the sun was warm on the pavements. I walked past Fowler's Fruit Shop and was quite glad it was already closed. Andy would be over at Lorette's, probably. His dad was coming round our house tonight. Mum was cooking him some fabulous meal or other. I think that's why she'd wanted me to push off to Mike's, actually.

I'd managed to reduce the time I spent thinking about Andy from twelve hours a day to about eleven and a half. I'd been watching lots of funny videos and all the laughing was doing me good. I could listen to Lorette telling me how wonderful Andy was without terrible things happening to my insides. I was quite pleased with myself, actually. I reckoned I deserved a gold star for bravery.

Ginger Mike opened the door without switching his Walkman off, and bowed low as I entered.

"Hi, Mike," I said. "Don't tell me — you forgot I was coming."

Mike's mum was rattling away at her word processor in the corner, and his gran was watching TV. She often stays with them and she beamed when she saw me. She's quite old, Ginger Mike's gran. Apparently his mum was a late baby, too.

Whereas my gran's a real raver. They call her the Belle of Battersea. I haven't ever told you much about her, have I? Still, it's a bit late to start on all that now. My gran's life story would take all night. And it's definitely a naughty story — a Parental Guidance Only Certificate.

"Hello, Silky!" I said. Everybody calls Ginger Mike's grandma Silky. I can't remember why. It's really nice. I'd like to have a special name when I'm a grandma. I don't want actually to be called Grandma. It's too grand, somehow.

"Why, Jane!" she said. "Haven't seen you for ages. Turn that blessed din off, Mike!"

Mike switched the TV off. But he was still listening to his Walkman, and singing from time to time.

"Hark at him," said his gran. "You'd think he was a half-wit. And look at Stella," she beamed across at Ginger Mike's mum busy with her word processor. "She's writing a letter to the newspaper again. I tell her she shouldn't, but she gets these bees in her bonnet. It's about this railway embankment they're trying to save."

"Save from what?"

"The developers. They want to build a block of flats there or something. But there's this fellow — forget his name — he's started a sort of nature reservation or whatever it's called, there. Three thousand varieties of wild flower, he's got there, you know."

"Three hundred," corrected Ginger Mike's mum, without moving her eyes from the screen. "Get Jane a Coke, Mike."

It would be nice to be able to have a Coke

without worrying about the bubbles going up or down the wrong way, or burping or hiccuping at the wrong moment or looking a bit of a twit. It was nice being in Ginger Mike's house where it was all friendly and relaxed. I felt happy.

"Wish I could get about a bit more," grumbled Mike's gran. "I'd be off down there picking all them wild flowers."

"You're not supposed to pick them, Mum!" Mike's mum explained. "That's the whole point of a nature reserve."

"What! Not pick them? Why ever not? Wouldn't do them any harm. Nice bunch o" buttercups, cheer us all up, they would."

Ginger Mike's cassette came to an end and he unplugged himself and went to fetch the Cokes.

"How are you?" I asked Mike's gran. "Have you been keeping well?"

My mum always taught me to ask people how they are. I'm quite well brought up, really. It's not my mum's fault I'm such a slob and a coward and an idiot. She's tried her best with me. The trouble is, my natural awfulness just shines through.

"I'm not too bad, thanks, Jane," said Mike's gran. "Me arthritis gives me gip now and then, but they've got me on this new miracle drug now, and the relief, well, it's marvellous. I'm a new woman."

"How fantastic! What is it?"

"What's it called?" Mike's gran pondered. "Ah yes. Steroids. That's it. Like what they give to them athletes."

I went hot. I went cold. The room sort of whirled around. I looked at Ginger Mike. He looked at me.

"Oh God!" I burst out. "Could that have been it, Mike?"

"Don't take the Lord's name in vain, dear. You never know when you might be bumping into him," said Mike's gran. But we weren't listening. I was staring at Mike and he was staring at me. I could see his hands beginning to shake. He went pale, then red, then pale again. It was like watching traffic lights change.

"Don't say anything!" he whispered, but his mum's ears are so sharp, she can hear what people are saying in the next house. She may have tennis elbow, but there's nothing wrong with her hearing.

"What have you done now, wretched boy?" she demanded, getting up from the word processor and fixing Mike with an awful glare. Mike shook.

"Nothing!" he pleaded. "Nothing, Mum. Honest." "Come on, Jane." She turned to me. "You're a sensible girl. What's he done?"

I looked at Mike and shook my head. This was too important to keep quiet about. It could be the way to clear Lorette's name.

"You know Lorette?" I said to Mike's mum. "You know about how she was up for those athletics trials and she had a drugs test and it was positive and she was disqualified and everything?"

"Yes," said Mike's mum. "Silly girl!"

"No!" I shouted. "It wasn't her fault. She's never done anything wrong. Only Mike — well — he gave her a couple of pills just before the race, because she had a headache. He thought they were headache pills. He took them from your bathroom cabinet — " at this point Ginger Mike hid behind

190

the curtains " — but I was thinking maybe they were Silky's."

"I told you, Stella!" said Ginger Mike's gran, pounding the arm of her chair. "I told you I was a few pills short! I knew I wasn't wrong!"

"All right, Mum. All right." Ginger Mike's mum scratched her head, and looked worried. "Michael!" she said in a very serious voice. The curtains twitched.

"Michael is not here," said Ginger Mike's voice. "This is his answering service. If you have a message, please speak after the — "

Ginger Mike's mum crossed the room in two strides and hauled him out from behind the curtains by his ear. Then she belted him quite hard across the backside. He looked surprised, and very embarrassed. I tried hard not to laugh. The whole thing was so farcical. But on the other hand, it was deadly serious. Life seems to be rather like that, I reckon. Even the most deadly serious moments have their comic side. Especially when Ginger Mike's involved.

"What have you been up to, you idiot?" His mum sort of shook him.

"He only takes aspirins," I said quickly. "In case any of us has headaches at school. He wants to be a chemist when he grows up."

"That's the first I've heard of it," said his mum.

"Don't be too hard on the lad," said his gran. "I remember now, they weren't in their proper bottle. I just brought a few with me when I stayed with you that time. You remember. It was only last week or something."

191

"I remember," said Ginger Mike's mum grimly. Then she sat Ginger Mike down, picked up the phone and dialled a number. It was Lorette's folks.

She explained what we'd discovered: that Mike had taken some steroid tablets from his mum's medicine chest, and given them to Lorette, and that was probably the answer to the whole stupid mystery. I could hear Lorette's mum kind of squealing with joy at the other end. Then Ginger Mike's mum started to apologise for him, but it seemed that Lorette's mum was so delighted to have the whole thing cleared up, that she didn't blame Mike at all. I reckon he got off lightly, come to think of it.

After Ginger Mike's mum had given him one hell of a talking to, she went off to a meeting and his gran fell asleep in a chair. Mike and I watched a science fiction movie on TV. He didn't join in with the baddies like he usually does, and he didn't *zap* or *pow* me the whole evening. I suppose he'd learnt his lesson. The movie was quite boring really, but I managed to think of Andy Fowler only once, and that was only about how pleased he'd be that Lorette's drugs test was all cleared up. I burped quite a lot because of the Coke, but of course it didn't matter.

When I got home, Andy Fowler's dad was still there. He doesn't look all that like Andy, but he has the same smile. As I walked in, he gave me a grin, and it was a bit strange, for a moment, to recognise that smile. It was almost as if he'd stolen it. Which is silly really, because it was Andy's dad's long before it was Andy's.

"Hey!" I said. "Guess what! Mike gave Lorette the steroids! He got them from his mum's bathroom cabinet. They were his gran's — for her arthritis."

Mum sort of stood stock-still and clapped her hand over her mouth.

"Oh no!" she said. "I meant to ring up Mike's mum and ask about that, days ago. How stupid of me! I clean forgot!"

"Head like a sieve," said Andy's dad. "It's those aluminium saucepans. Tell you what — when's your birthday? I'll buy you a set of stainless steel ones."

"What are you talking about, Tony Fowler?" asked Mum, in a funny kind of playful voice, as if he was a little boy.

"Aluminium saucepans," he said. "They can make you go prematurely ga-ga. It's the aluminium, you know. Poisons the brain."

"It's too late," said Mum. "I'm hopeless. Jane knows what I'm like. I can hardly remember your name, even. What did you say it was, again?"

They laughed, and Mum poured out some more wine, and I began to feel I was in the way, a little. Maybe I should tactfully retire to bed and leave the field free for a bit of romance over the candlelit coffee cups.

"Andy'll be thrilled about this," said his dad, rubbing his wine glass against his stubble. Mum likes men with a bit of stubble on their faces. I think she must have told him this at some stage, because I'd noticed that he didn't shave quite as much as usual these days. I hated stubble, myself.

It must be like kissing a hedgehog. I tried not to listen to what he was saying, about Andy. I tried hard to concentrate on the stubble. But it was no good. "He's really gone on your mate Lorette," he went on, grinning at me. Somehow I managed to grin back. Heroic, that's me.

"I know. And she's crazy about him."

" 'S funny," said Andy's dad, giving me a rather long, strange look, "but I always thought it was you he fancied."

"Oh, no." I looked down at the table top, and traced around the pattern on the tablecloth with my fingertips. "It was Lorette."

"Not always it wasn't," said Andy's dad. "Shame, really. I mean, Lorette's a great girl, don't get me wrong, I'm not saying she isn't. Only it would be, well, sort of cosy if you and Andy had got it together, don't you think?"

He grinned and waved his wine glass around the room to indicate cosiness. I got up and shook my head. It all sounded a little bit too cosy for me.

"I'm off to bed, then," I said. "Goodnight."

I was a bit embarrassed, saying goodnight to them like that. I was definitely in the way. It must be hard to settle down to a romantic evening on the sofa if your teenage daughter is likely to come bursting into the room at any moment.

I don't know when Tony Fowler left, but when I went down for a glass of water at midnight, Mum was sitting by herself in the rocking chair, rocking to and fro to some very quiet music and smiling a secret smile.

I blew her a kiss, and she blew one back. She

deserved all the happiness that was going. For the first time I realised how much better it was that my love-life should go catastrophically wrong, and Mum's go right. That made me feel a hell of a lot better. I managed to get back off to sleep again without thinking of Andy Fowler at all. It's a pity there isn't a Duke of Edinburgh's Award for Teen-age Girls Recovering from Broken Hearts. I tell you, I'd be right in line for one of those. The big shiny gold variety.

20

I suppose it was about two months later that
Lorette's birthday came round. We organised a surprise party for her in our den in the cemetery. I
arranged to meet Wayne there early and get everything ready. Then Sudeshna and Ginger Mike were
going to turn up bringing the crisps and food and
drink from Sudeshna's shop. Finally Andy was
going to lure Lorette over, only she wouldn't know
we'd all be there, hiding behind Cara Giovanezza's
tombstone, ready to pounce out shouting, SUR-
PRISE!

As I walked down Church Street, I thought what
a lot had happened in the past few weeks. It had
certainly been a good time for Lorette. She'd been
cleared of the drugs business and the athletics
people said she could compete in the trials next
year. She'd still be under seventeen. Miss Andrews
said it might be a good idea to wait for a year in
any case, as Lorette would benefit from an extra
year's growing and training and it wasn't a good
idea to push young athletes too far, too soon.

So Lorette had been taking it easy — well, by her
standards. She'd still organised a sponsored roller-
skating disco in aid of saving the rain forests, and
managed to get top marks in three subjects in the
school exams. I grinned to myself. Lorette was
certainly a star. And next year she'd be even more

of a star. She might even be the British 400 metres champion in her age group! I felt proud. I felt like her agent or something.

She'd also had some great times with Andy. They were almost inseparable these days. After work he'd go round to her house and have supper with her family, most days. But his dad wasn't lonely. Because he'd come round our house and have supper with my mum! Yes. It was love's young dream. Or rather, love's middle-aged dream. Mind you, my mum was looking younger and younger these days. I almost felt responsible for her, sometimes, when she skipped about and sang to herself. I was going to have to give her a good talking-to, soon: about not being taken in by men.

I got to the cemetery early. Nobody was about. So I sat on a stone and looked at Cara Giovanezza's tombstone again. Had she had heartaches? I bet she had. These Italians were passionate so-and-sos. I smiled, remembering the passion fruit that Andy had given me. He should've given me ugli fruit really. I grinned again. Actually I wasn't looking too bad these days. I'd managed to keep my weight down with lots of self-defence classes.

Then I remembered Larry Payne. It all seemed to have happened years ago. Larry had been lucky not to get into worse trouble about Wayne's injury. It had been one of his friends who'd had the knife, just as Wayne had said, so Larry got off with a severe warning. He ignored me at school for the rest of the term. But anyway, the sixth form hardly bothered to come into school for most of the summer term anyway, what with exams and everything. I shook my head, not able to believe how stupid I'd been over him. He didn't even look dishy any more.

I picked a daisy and pulled off the petals one by one, scattering them on the grass.

"Hey! He loves you!" said a voice right behind me. It was Wayne. I threw the daisy away, shaking my head.

"No he doesn't!" I said.

"She loves me, she loves me not," said Wayne, picking another.

"Ah well. Can't have everything."

"Wayne . . . "

"Yeah?"

"I was just thinking about old times. You know, when you were in that fight with Larry and everything."

"Hey, sister! Don't think about that! That's ancient history."

"I never thanked you properly."

"What for? I didn't do nothin'."

"Yes you did! Of course you did. You stood up for me. You defended me. You even got hurt for me. You were my knight in shining armour. And I never even said thank you."

"Come on, Jane! Forget it. You'll have me in tears, now. I'm too big to cry, y'know."

"No, but really, Wayne. I never said much to you. But I was really grateful."

"I know why you never said anything."

"Why?"

" 'Cos Lorette was on at you all the time about me. I know. She's got no tact, that girl. I know the things she was sayin'. About how gorgeous I was and you'd better fall down and worship me or else."

I laughed. But I felt a little bit uneasy. This was almost the truth, after all.

"Listen, sister," said Wayne. "I want you to know that I was a little, well, a little crazy about you for a while. But I've got myself sorted out now and I'm takin' out a girl from down Mildmay Avenue."

"What?" I jumped right up and stared at him. "Tell me more, Wayne!" I'd never been so glad to hear anything in my life. Although, funnily enough, there was a little tiny bit of regret that he wasn't crazy about me any more. A little bit of regret and a lot of relief. Now nobody was crazy about me: nobody at all.

Wayne told me about his girl. Her name was Georgia Neve and she was a gorgeous redhead with skin like white satin — according to Wayne. He may have been exaggerating a little. I was really pleased for him, and I gave him a big hug to congratulate him. Just then Mike and Sudeshna arrived.

"Hey! Stop that!" shouted Mike. "No Sex Please, We're British! Where's the ghostly outfits?"

Wayne had brought some sheets and masks and things and the idea was, we'd jump out from behind a tombstone and give Lorette the scare of her life. Actually, I didn't think it would be all that scary, in broad daylight on a sunny day. But Ginger Mike was already dressing himself up as a vampire. It kind of suited him, actually. Only he made a slightly too friendly vampire. The sort that would secretly prefer tomato ketchup and blood oranges.

Sudeshna threw a sheet over her head and started making some quite creepy noises. Wayne put on a werewolf mask.

"Hey!" I said, "Wayne! Now I could really fancy you!"

He chased me round the tombstone and pretended to bite a hole in my neck. Then I had to dress up. There was a witch's hat with a spider hanging from it. I quite fancied that. Plus I had brought my make-up bag and mirror and I gave us all ghoulish eyes, outlined with black sparkly kohl.

Then, we hid the food and drink behind a tree, and at the appointed time, we all crouched down behind the tombstone. Sudeshna kept giggling because of Ginger Mike's non-stop Dracula jokes, and Wayne's mask kept crackling, but by six-thirty we were ready and waiting. Far away between the trees, a couple came wandering towards us. It was Andy and Lorette. Their arms were round each other, and they were whispering sweet nothings as they came. Andy was in on the surprise, of course, so he led her gradually over in our direction.

Soon they were right up close. Lorette looked up at the sunlight filtering down through the trees.

"It's so beautiful and peaceful, here," She gave a sort of happy sigh. "Listen to that bird, Andy."

"SURPRISE!!!!" we all yelled in unison, leaping up from behind the tomb. Lorette screamed and then got hysterics. She couldn't stop laughing.

"Hey! Hey! Pat me on the back!" she shouted. "Or I'm gonna choke to death!"

Eventually we all calmed down and Sudeshna got out a mouth-watering picnic of stuff she had brought from her dad's shop. There were crisps, and peanuts, and cheese, and tomatoes, and cucumber, and hummus and taramasalata, and crackers, and chocolate biscuits, and Coke and apple juice. We all gorged ourselves. After all, it was Lorette's birthday treat.

Then we sang Happy Birthday and lit a candle. Only it looked a bit silly in the sunlight. Lorette blew it out and the wisp of black smoke rose up into the sky and vanished. Then we all kissed her and gave her presents. Well, everybody except Ginger Mike kissed her.

"I do not kiss," he said. "But I am prepared to place my head beneath your foot, madam."

I gave Lorette a book about the rain forests. Wayne gave her a Walkman — well, it was part of a present from her whole family, really. Sudeshna gave her some jasmine oil in a little brown bottle, and Andy had given her a gold chain for her neck. She was already wearing it, and it gleamed beautifully against her brown skin. Ginger Mike gave her a cassette called "Music of the Andes". She listened to it for a while with her eyes closed, and then gave it to me.

"This is far out, Jane," she said. "Just listen to those pan pipes!"

I put the Walkman on and settled back.

The most wonderful sound I'd ever heard came wafting into my ears. It was distant and echoey and magical. It spoke of haunted places, of high waterfalls, of huge towering trees with creepers hanging down from the canopy; of snow-covered mountains and weird birds and animals calling to

201

each other across a purple sky. As I listened, I knew right away that one day, I had to go there.

Yes. I would pack up a few things in a rucksack, wave goodbye to my mum (safe in the hands of Tony Fowler), and I'd be off to explore the world. Starting with the Andes. That's what I was going to do. I knew, at last, what I wanted. The music changed now to a throbbing jungle sound. I could almost hear snakes sliding through the undergrowth and the nocturnal howls of monkeys.

"This is great, Mike!" I said. "This jungle one."

Mike stood up to his full height (getting on for six feet, these days) and beat his breast like a gorilla and howled.

"Shush, Mike!" said Lorette. "Someone's gonna hear and we'll be kicked out."

Mike turned towards me and put on an expression of Neanderthal lust.

"Me Tarzan!" he grunted. "You — woman."

"You — pathetic twit!" I grunted back. "Me Jane!"

He lunged at me, but I rolled aside and he fell into the grass. I went on listening to the music, and everybody quietened down a little.

Andy and Lorette were leaning against each other and holding hands. I smiled at them. It didn't hurt any more. It hadn't hurt for ages. I was so glad that Lorette was happy — and that Andy was, too. I'd got bored with heartbreak. It just gets better by itself in the end. Sitting here with my mates in the late summer sun, after a really great picnic, was just fabulous. What more could I have wanted?

Nobody was crazy about me, and I wasn't crazy about anyone either. How fantastic, the freedom that gave you! I was going to stay as far away as possible from the idea of boyfriends, for as long as I could. Unless of course Tarzan turned up. And I think even then I'd have to send him away to college to learn how to cook and sew and things. You won't catch me turning into a household slave like so many mums are, even in these modern days.

I was going round the world. To hell with love. I closed my eyes in perfect happiness, and just opened them once more to make sure they were all still there, all still all right: Wayne chewing a stalk of grass and smiling up at the sky, dreaming of his Georgia, perhaps; not looking at me like a hurt dog any more, thank goodness. Sudeshna clearing up after the picnic, throwing away the crumbs and brushing bits of grass off her skirt. Mike lying flat on his back with the werewolf mask on, like something from a horror movie taking a holiday. Andy and Lorette all intertwined.

Then I looked up at the angel on the tomb. We're only here on earth for such a short time. We must take care of each other and help our friends to be happy or what's life for? I closed my eyes. They were all all right. I gave myself up to the music. To hell with romance. Give me friendship any day. And give me the Andes. Gift-wrapped, preferably.

When I got home, an hour or so later, Mum and Tony Fowler were starting to paint the kitchen.

"No, let me!" he was saying, trying to pull her down off the ladder.

"Listen!" shouted Mum. "I managed perfectly

well on my own for years, thank you very much, Tony Fowler. I can climb stepladders, believe it or not, and not fall off!"

"Ah, but now I'm going to look after you!" he said with a laugh. I was standing in the hall. They hadn't even noticed me. "And whether you like it or not, mate, you're going to be cherished — cherished to death!"

Mum burst out laughing and fell into his arms. Quietly I went out again and closed the door without even a click. I can be as velvety as a spy when I really try.

I went out and walked round the park. There was just time before the gates were locked. The lake was glimmering silver in the twilight. I'd walk round it and then go home and ring the doorbell. Be tactful. Pretend I'd forgotten my key. I grinned to myself. It was as if Mum was the soppy teenager and I was the long-suffering parent. Let her have her fun. She deserved it.

The bell was ringing to warn people that the park gates were going to close very soon. I paused by the lake, and looked down into its shadowy depths. The dark face of myself looked up at me out of the water. Then I heard a sudden flap and flutter in the distance. It was the heron. The one Wayne had shown me on the island, that day long ago — the day of the Greenpeace Fair.

The bird's great angular wings sawed the air and up it rose: higher and higher, until it flew right above me, across the soft dark heads of the trees westwards into the last rays of the sun. I was glad I'd seen it again. It seemed to complete a circle, somehow. And I was glad it was all right: strong and healthy and flying off into the unknown. Lucky bird. But I was a lucky bird, too. It was time to go home.

Also in
Lions Tracks

To order direct from the publisher, just tick the titles you want and fill in the order form on the last page.

All these books are available at your local bookshop or newsagent, or can be ordered from the publishers.

To order direct from the publishers just tick the titles you want and fill in the form below:

Name _____

Address _____

_____

Send to: Collins Children's Cash Sales
PO Box 11
Falmouth
Cornwall
TR10 9EN

Please enclose a cheque or postal order or debit my Visa/Access –

Credit card no:

Expiry date:

Signature:

– to the value of the cover price plus:

UK: 80p for the first book, and 20p per copy for each additional book ordered to a maximum charge of £2.00.

BFPO: 80p for the first book and 20p per copy for each additional book.

Overseas and Eire: £1.50 for the first book, £1.00 for the second book, thereafter 30p per book.

Lions Tracks